BEAT THE DRUM SLOWLY

BEAT THE DRUM SLOWLY

by

Dave Waldo

Dales Large Print Books
Long Preston, North Yorkshire,
BD23 4ND, England.

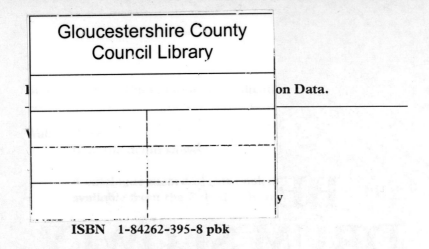

I   on Data.

ISBN   1-84262-395-8 pbk

First published in Great Britain in 1963
by Ward Lock and Company Limited

Copyright © 1961 by Dave Waldo

Cover illustration © Faba by arrangement with
Norma Editorial S.A

The moral right of the author has been asserted

Published in Large Print 2005 by arrangement with
Dave Waldo, care of Rupert Crew Limited

Dales Large Print is an imprint of Library Magna Books Ltd.

Printed and bound in Great Britain by
T.J. (International) Ltd., Cornwall, PL28 8RW

To Joanna and Robin

CHAPTER ONE

The first time I ever set eyes on Dan Maffrey was way down in the dry desert country of what was then the New Mexico territory, in 1878 still a mighty wild and lonesome place. But no more wild and lonesome than I was on that early Spring day.

I was hunkered down in the lee of a big chunk of rock and trying to tie a bandanna round a messed-up right hand when I took a look down trail. Now there's only one thing that raises a dust cloud like the one I could see in the distance and that's a trail-herd on the move. The dust-cloud raised by a posse is smaller. Nothing special about a trail-herd moving north in those days it's true but this one was moving where, so far as I knew, trail-herds weren't known. They usually stuck like ants to the Chisholm or the Goodnight trail and this one was way over to the west of those well-known cattle roads.

Now on that occasion it seemed mighty important for me to move out of that bit of desert just about as fast as possible and it struck me then that a job with a north-bound herd might be just what I wanted. The herd was several miles south of my rock so I just settled down to wait for them. I built myself a cigarette with my left hand and watched the blood soaking through the neckerchief I'd managed to tie around my right.

I smoked and waited, and about an hour later the herd was nearly level with my camp. It was time to make my play if I wanted a job so I climbed onto Bessie, my cayuse, and rode leisurely down towards the herd. It wasn't very big. Not more, I figured, than about seven-eight hundred head. The drovers must have seen me coming because three of them bunched together and were waiting as I came up.

They were hard-looking hombres, their shirts and chaps thickly powdered with white dust, their neck-pieces over their mouths and their eyes puffy and red. As I got near one of them said, 'What do you want, stranger?' 'Work,' I said. 'Mebbe you could use an extra hand if you're heading north.' They just sat their horses and looked at me as if I'd insulted them. Then a second one, a humped-up, over-heated gent, said sourly, 'We don't want no extra hands. Vamos!'

A fourth drover joined them at that point.

He was a big man and he sat a big horse, a black. He stared at me and I noticed that he had very bright, hard, blue eyes.

'What goes on?' he said.

'This hombre says he's lookin' for work,' said the man who'd first spoken. 'I reckon he's lookin' for trouble. He can mosey on.'

I felt the big man's eyes staring at me, especially at my bandaged hand.

'What's wrong with your hand, mister?'

'Nothing that a little time won't cure,' I said. 'It was bit by a bee.'

'Git movin',' said the one who'd already told me to be on my way.

'Wait,' said the big hombre, 'I reckon we could do with another hand. You know anything about cattle?'

'I was raised on the Texas plains,' I said. 'I've been with cattle since I was knee-high to a grasshopper.'

'You're hired,' said the big blue-eyed man. 'It's thirty a month an' found. You got a name?'

'Yes,' I said, 'My name's Ross. Johnny Ross.'

The red-faced hombre who'd told me to vamoose had difficulty with his mouth. It just went wide open like a hooked fish, so I figured he'd heard my name before.

He said, 'I've heard tell of you, mister. You're just a goddam gunslinger.'

'Mebbe,' I said, a bit coldly. 'But not at the moment.'

The big man who'd done the hiring butted in then.

'My name's Maffrey,' he said. 'Dan Maffrey.' He gestured towards the others. The red-faced one was called Abe Somers. The other two were Mitch Fenton, short, heavy-set, cruel-faced, and Willamette, pale-haired, pale-eyed. No other name. Maffrey didn't seem to know them very well and I sensed a sort of atmosphere about the whole bunch that spelled some kind of trouble.

'I still say we can git along without him,' said the one called Mitch Fenton sullenly.

Maffrey stared at him for a long moment without speaking.

'When we left the Nueces,' he said at last, 'you all agreed that I should boss this drive.'

'Yes,' said the one called Willamette, 'an' look where it's got us. Plumb into the middle of a God-forsaken desert, with the cattle half-dead an' no water for miles.'

I could feel the tension building up all round us, with all the hate and suspicion centring on Maffrey from the other three.

'It was a risk we had to take,' said Maffrey

coldly. 'Any other trail would have meant a week or more longer. The offer to buy runs out on the 15th May.'

'Better lose the sale than lose the cattle,' said Abe Somers belligerently. 'There's no other buyers in Colorado.'

'I contracted to sell to Morgan Lewis an' when you asked to throw in with me you agreed to bide by the same agreement.' Maffrey was quiet but his ice-blue eyes looked dangerous.

The other three just stood there staring their hatred at him but something about this Dan Maffrey kept them quiet, and after a bit they split up and went back to the herd. I noticed the one called Willamette pulling hard on the bit and then lashing his cayuse with a quirt when it got restive.

'You'd better let me have a look at that hand,' Maffrey said, and climbed slowly out of his saddle.

I found myself unwinding the blood-stained bandanna without a murmur. He stared at the bloody mess that Jed Benson's slug had made of my right hand. Then without speaking he went over to his hoss and dug around his saddle-bag. He came back with a bottle of Old Crow and a roll of bandage. He took my hand just above the wrist, uncorked the whisky with his teeth and began to pour it very slowly over the hole in my palm. It felt like someone had taken a red-hot poker to it. I just shut my eyes, gritted my teeth and wriggled around a bit. When he'd done he mopped up the wound with a piece of bandage and then bound it up with more bandaging.

'Seen worse,' he said dubiously. 'Reckon if you keep it clean it'll be all right.'

'What're you aimin' to do about the cattle?' I said. 'Yore pardner wasn't so far out when he said there was no water for miles.'

'There should be water not more than ten miles on,' he said. 'We'll get through somehow, come hell or high water.'

I said 'Yup' – a mite dubiously maybe and went over to my horse. I climbed into the saddle and rode round to where Maffrey stood. He said, 'You ride out on the left flank. We'll push 'em on till sundown and see what the morning brings up.'

I rode on down to the place he'd given me. And so the drive was on. And on through high noon and land as empty and desolate as hell itself, with nothing to break the desolation but some clumps of mesquite and a stand of saguaros like dead men's fingers pointing up into the aching blue sky.

The change when it came was sudden. One moment there was nothing by the glare of the westering sun and the big blue bowl of the sky. And then staring ahead I saw that over the northern ranges there were clouds, big bunched-up masses. They looked dark and angry and moving up on us fast. I thought I saw lightning forking down out of them. Then sure enough I heard a good loud rumble of thunder. It didn't look good, not at all. Cow-critters spook all to hell in a bad thunderstorm and this one was shaping up like the grand-daddy of all. And I've seen some. Dan Maffrey came riding up then out of the dust cloud on my right. 'Looks like trouble head,' he shouted. 'We'll try bunchin 'em until the storm's over.'

He rode off and in the big quiet that seemed to have crept up on us I could hear him shouting to the others. I watched him ride up towards the head of the herd and knew it was time to ride in and help bunch the cattle. It was getting darker every minute and there were lightning flashes coming zig-a-zag from all sides. Then the rain began. Steady at first, in large drops falling leisurely-like and hissing on the hot stony desert. It was darker now than the inside of a cow's belly and the rain increased to a downpour. I rode in towards the herd. It suddenly looked larger than seven-eight hundred head. Horns were up and eyeballs rolling. My cayuse began to dance – always a sure sign of trouble, and then the heavens above just seemed to open up and empty their stored-up poison on top of us. There was a crash like the world's big guns in action, a huge white glaring flash and a cloudburst of rain. Bessie went up on her hind legs and as I fought her down I had one terrible glimpse of the herd break up and stampede. They seemed to move forward, like one giant cow, into a lumbering run, bellowing insanely with fear, as more gigantic lightning flashes danced off their rain-soaked backs. I thought I saw Maffrey once but was too busy trying to keep up with the herd as it ran. And run it did, faster than any stampeding herd I've seen. And then one vast flash saved my life. It lit up the whole scene. Ahead the masses of cattle seemed to hesitate and then disappear. The bellowing and roaring seemed for a moment to increase. I sensed rather than saw what had happened and reined in hard. I was just in time. Another flash showed nothing at all three yards from where we stood. The herd had gone over a canyon rim. I waited trembling for another glimpse and had it.

Way over to my right a few cows stood disconsolately. The rest had been swallowed up. The thunder was rolling away south-west now. For a moment I thought I could hear a distant howling and crying and then there was nothing, except that it got lighter and I could see things again.

I looked back over the path the herd had taken. A long way over north of where I was I could see two figures on horseback. A third form way down trail was angling over towards them. There had to be another one somewhere and then I saw him coming into sight from way back. Even at that distance you could see it was Dan Maffrey.

I rode down towards him and when I reached him I dismounted. He didn't say a word for some time, just halted in his tracks and stared at me.

'Where's the herd?' he said at last, dry and husky.

'Gone,' I said, 'over the canyon rim.'

The news staggered him as I knew it would. He was a man to feel responsible for that kind of thing. It's the good who feel guilty. And Maffrey looked sick with guilt.

'The others owned a part of that herd,' he said.

'They can't blame you, mister, for an act

of God.'

'They can, Ross, an' they sure will.'

I looked round and saw the other three riding towards us in a tight little bunch. They didn't seem to be saying much and as they rode up I could see that they looked as grim as hell. They spread out a bit as they reined in and I could smell trouble in the air.

Mitch Fenton just said, 'Well?'

And Maffrey had nothing to say, just stood there, his shoulders loose, not looking at them.

'Every goddam thing we owned was in that herd,' said Abe Somers.

'Yes,' said Maffrey. 'I know. I'll do what I can to repay you.'

'Repay,' said Fenton, his face all twisted up in a big ugly sneer of hate. 'It's us'll do the repaying, mister.' And before you could wink he'd drawn his Colts, smooth and fast, with more speed than anything I'd seen for a long time. 'Climb off that hoss, mister,' Fenton was saying. 'Slow and easy-like an' toss your gun over to me.'

'The same goes for you, stranger,' said Willamette to me.

So Maffrey climbed off his hoss and dropped his gun way out in front of him. I climbed slowly out of the saddle too. Wasn't anything else I could do. My right hand was all shot up and my left had always led a gentlemanly sort of life, with nothing much to do save take the air and bask in the sun. And my gun was in my saddle-bag anyway. We all stood there in a quiet unnatural kind of group and I watched Fenton, who was by a long way the most dangerous of the three, work himself into a decision.

'Yes,' he said at last. 'We'll do the repaying, Mister Maffrey. You've made fools out of us too long. Reckon you didn't figure what sort of folks you were joining up with back in the Nueces. Just three quiet hombres who wanted to sell their cattle up north. So you just kinda took command an' led us into this mess.'

Dan Maffrey didn't say anything. Just stood there looking a mite pale an' more than a mite dignified.

'Get it over with, Mitch,' said Abe Somers. 'Ain't no call for a big pow-wow.'

I reckoned it was time I said something. There was the sour smell of death in the air.

'You ain't going to shoot a man in cold blood,' I said.

'I aim to do just that,' said Mitch Fenton. 'An' not a man but two men.'

'That means you, mister,' said Willamette, with his usual display of special feeling for me.

Surprisingly Abe Somers said, 'Reckon we might leave him out of it.'

Fenton's reply to this was swift. 'Don't be a goddam fool, Abe. We can't leave any witnesses around.'

'All right, all right,' mumbled Somers.

My mind began to move fast. I had no particular desire for an early death. All three of them were staring now at Maffrey and looking at Fenton I could see he was trying to work himself up to that high point where he could raise the gun and shoot Maffrey down. It isn't as easy to do as some folks think. It was my only chance and I took it. There was a fist-sized rock just at my feet. I bent down, grabbed it and threw it straight at Fenton's head. Without even waiting to see whether it hit him I whirled and jumped for my pony. It was only two yards behind me. As I jumped into the saddle I let out a yell that woke the pony into a frenzy of bucking. I was dimly aware of them scattering around me, a gun roared only inches away it seemed and then the pony lit out faster than a jack-rabbit. There were two more shots but by this time we were out of range in the tangle of rocks way over to the west of the trail. I got in among them and twisted and turned until I judged I was safe from pursuit. Then I dismounted and with some difficulty rolled myself a smoke. I felt kind of mean about leaving Dan Maffrey to face those three killers alone but there hadn't been much choice. I'd been lucky and I decided I'd probably stay lucky. They weren't likely to waste time hunting for me but would head on north, I figured. I'd wait a while and then go see what they'd done to Dan Maffrey. It wasn't any of my business and none of them, not even this Dan Maffrey, meant anything to me. But still I felt I owed it to him to go see that he wasn't just left for the coyotes to howl over. After all he'd tried to something to my poor old right hand.

CHAPTER TWO

About an hour later I rode back to the canyon rim, with both eyes open. At first in the fading light of day I could see nothing. Mitch Fenton, Somers and Willamette had gone. Then I spotted what looked like a body a few yards away from where we'd originally stopped. I rode up and climbed out of the saddle. It was Dan Maffrey all right, huddled over on his right side. I went to him and laid him out flat. Someone had shot him through the body, the whole front of his shirt was soaked with blood. And then just as I was about to get up and look for rocks to pile on him I saw one of his eyelids flicker. I quickly bent down and put my ear to his chest. At first I could hear nothing and then it came, the unmistakable heart beat of a man still alive.

I ran back to my pony and grabbed my cantina. I whipped off my bandanna, moistened it with water and wiped the dirt off Maffrey's face. I didn't know how badly shot he was and didn't want to take any risks. If I

23

could get him some kind of help maybe he'd have a chance. The country was all new to me but I thought there'd be some ranch down below the plateau.

I got my saddle and put it under his head. Then I pulled his shirt off and had a look at the wound. It was bad, mighty bad. A big hole in his right shoulder, the blood still pouring out of it. I got a spare shirt out of his saddle-bag, washed away the blood and plugged the hole as best I could. I then discovered that he'd been shot twice more, probably when he was lying face down in the desert sand. They must have been jittery. One shot had just creased his left side below the ribs. The other had made a deeper furrow along his right arm. I did what I could for these and by then it was dark. I decided to sit it out till dawn. If he was still alive then, I'd pack him on his horse and look for help.

Once in the long night he came awake and croaked out one word, 'Water'. I gave him a few sips and he sighed and then I heard no more until dawn crept up on us in its usual pale way.

I judged it safe to light a fire then. I managed to rake together some manzanilla twigs and built up a small hot fire. I put a coffee pot on the fire to boil and then had a look at

24

Maffrey. He was in bad shape, the skin of his face drawn and pale, his breath uneven. I took the homemade bandage off the wound in his chest and then quickly put it back. It looked worse than before, red and inflamed round the edges and still oozing blood. I decided to risk giving him some coffee and when it was made I propped him up with my left arm and fed him some of the strong black brew. It worked better than I'd expected. His eyes opened and tried to focus on me.

'What's matter?' he said at last. 'What's happened?'

The words came out slow and painful and I figured it was no time for long conversations.

'Rest easy,' I said. 'Your pardners put a coupla slugs in you and lit out for parts unknown.'

His eyes seemed to come awake then and I knew by the glitter in them that he was mad clean through. He tried to say something but couldn't quite make it. 'Talk's doing you no good,' I said. 'Leave it till later.'

He tried again, however, and managed to get out two words – 'Money' and 'Belt'.

To oblige him I had a look, but his money belt, if that's what he was after, was gone.

He didn't say any more, just closed his eyes

and lay there breathing hard and looking like he was pretty close to old Death's door. It was going to be mighty risky trying to move him but he couldn't just lie there and die of starvation. The two mules and their loads had obviously gone off with Fenton and his two buddies. I drank some coffee and rolled a cigarette. By the time I was through with it I had made up my mind. I was going to get Maffrey onto his cayuse and look for some place where he could be tended.

I put out the fire by emptying what remained of the coffee on it. Then I got the two horses as close as possible. I put my saddle back on my mount and then set about the task of getting Maffrey off the ground and onto his pony. He was a big man and heavy. It took me a lot of time and a lot of sweat before I had him in the saddle. He was half-conscious and I managed to get him to rest both hands on the horn. Then I climbed onto Bessie and very slowly got away from the canyon rim.

It was already warm and I knew we had to make some kind of human habitation in a few hours or Maffrey would die. There was more chance of finding a small town or ranch by heading north, I figured. This meant getting down off the rimrock onto level ground. There was a whole lot of desert ahead and beyond the desert some big mountain peaks pushed up into the bright blue morning sky.

We skirted the rim for a time until we reached a down-grade track. It led down easily onto level ground, brown and dry and mighty unfriendly. Before setting out across the flats I gave Maffrey another swallow from the canteen. Then we pushed on through the rising morning heat. I could feel the sweat trickling down my cheeks and neck and soon the ponies started to lather. We rode on. And on and on for what seemed a lot of time. Maffrey let out a kind of moaning noise from time to time but there wasn't much I could do about it. I figured he was in a pretty bad way and wondered if he'd last. I've seen all kinds of folks in my wanderings on the frontier and you just can't tell which is the surviving kind. For my money it's the small and thin that last longest, so long as they don't get in the way of a bullet. And Dan Maffrey was a big hombre, tall and solid. The heat got worse and worse as we rode on and it was with a sigh of relief that I spotted a clump of live oak not far ahead of us. It was about time to rest. We'd been in the saddle for over four hours.

We reached the trees and I beat around a bit to scare off any rattlers that might be having a quiet snooze in the shade. Then I got Maffrey down out of his saddle and laid him out under an oak. He looked worse than ever and I realised that there was only one thing to do. I'd have to ride on alone and look for a house where he could get some tending. I gave him some more water and then I wiped off the mouths of the horses. I left the rest with Maffrey. Then I rode again out into the desert.

I rode easy. There was the horse to think of. The hours went by. Time was a patch of cholla cactus, a white skeleton, a rock pile rising out of the brown and stony flats. I circled it and found myself on an east-west trail, not well used but enough. By burros as the tracks told me. Could lead to a Mexican adobe. I mopped my face with an end of my bandanna. I rode east. The trail rose slowly over a ridge and petered out in the yard of a small Mexican adobe. Maybe I was in luck after all. A half-naked brown-skinned boy was playing in the dirt outside the door. I rode up and called out. A woman came to the door staring out at me with the suspicion they all feel, and maybe rightly, for all gringos.

'What you want?' Her voice was flat with fear and doubt. I told her, using what Spanish words I knew. About Maffrey being shot up and needing help. While I was talking, her husband came over the far ridge of the valley and rode in warily. The woman chattered to him swiftly. He listened, his face impassive, his black eyes fixed unwinking on me. At last he stopped her with a word and addressed me with the courtesy that these folk seem to drink in with their mother's milk.

'We go help the wounded one, señor.'

That was all and a couple of minutes later we were on our way back with water.

When we reached Dan Maffrey I thought he was a goner. He lay there white and twisted-looking with a shaft of sunlight breaking through onto his face. The Mexican, whose name I'd discovered was Jesus Garcia, was off his mount and ministering to Maffrey before you could say 'knife'. He got him propped up and gave him something out of a bottle that I guessed was tequila. Some of the colour came back into his cheeks and Garcia strapped up the bullet wounds with long strips of cloth. Then he made a sign to me and we set about getting Maffrey on his horse. We got him back to the adobe in a couple of hours and the woman had a bed all fixed up in a woodshed out back. Then they fed him some kind of soup and pretty soon he was on his back and sleeping sound.

It was my turn after that. The woman had seen the blood-stained rag round my right hand and without a by-your-leave she whipped it off, washed out the wound and then poured tequila over it. It was like all hell itself let loose in my hand and arm and I saw her watching me with a tight sort of smile. So instead of letting out a yell I made a few faces at her and she drew back a pace or two. Then when she figured it was safe again she came back and put some kind of salve over the hole and the pain began to go. After that we had beans and tortillas and a big dish of stewed-up goat, all very hot and comforting. We smoked together and talked a bit and not once did either of them ask a single question about who we were or where we were bound. They gave me a mattress and I just lay down and went to sleep for what seemed like a thousand years.

We were there for thirteen days. The first four of them were a fight, a fight for the life of Dan Maffrey. And we won. Slowly but surely the holes began to mend. His colour came back and he began to sleep well and eat hearty. There wasn't much for me to do.

Jesus Garcia and his wife went off with their goats or worked in their maize and melon patches.

One morning I was sitting in the shade of the adobe looking out over the hills when a thought hit me. Life wasn't going to be any easier from now on than it had been for the past five years of fiddle-footed wandering in New Mexico and the Territory. One day the past was going to catch up with me. I'd go into a saloon and there'd be some hombre I'd met somewhere along the trail and he'd say, 'Johnny Ross, by grab,' and go for his gun. And how was Mister Ross to answer that one when his right hand couldn't properly hold a can of beans, let alone a Colt 45.

I looked down at the same right hand resting nice and peaceful. The Owens boys had made a neat job of it. It was twisted and useless. And then staring a mite gloomily at it, I remembered I'd got another hand somewhere and it was time for it to go to work. After all it had had things pretty easy for the past thirty years.

I got up and went into the lean-to where my saddlebag was cached. I took out my belt and gun and some oily rags and went back to my place in the sun. The gun hadn't been used

31

since I'd high-tailed it out of Newtown with one of the Owens boys dead on the floor of the Golden Nugget Saloon and the other two brothers with their pals roaring for my blood. I took it to pieces slowly, cleaned it and oiled it. It was a lovely piece of work, clean and dark and dangerous. It had been my closest friend for quite a spell and I wasn't giving up that friendship just yet. When I'd fitted it all together again I loaded it and then I stood up. The next part was going to be tricky and I didn't look forward to it. I strapped the gun belt on and shoved the Colt into the holster. I stood there quietly in the sunlight and looked for a target. The only thing that would do was a small boulder off to my left and about twenty yards away. I just stood there looking at it and sweating with nervousness. I tried to persuade myself it was the hot morning sun but it wasn't. I was just plain scared of trying to get that Colt out of its holster with my left hand.

And then someone coughed from just behind me. I whirled reaching for the gun in the good old way with my right hand. I might have been fishing for trout with a hammer for all the good I did. It was Dan Maffrey standing there looking mighty thin and gaunted up. He grinned and said, 'Howdy!'

I said, 'Good to see you on your pins again.'

'Feel kinda wobbly,' he replied. He came slowly down to where I stood with the Colt in my twisted hand.

'You'll have to start practising with your left, Johnny,' he said.

'I was figuring on something like that,' I replied.

'Good,' said Maffrey, giving me a long hard calculating kind of look. Then he just walked off back to his bed.

Well, I set about it there and then and, to cut this part of the story short, within three or four days I was making a fairly smooth draw with my good left hand and getting about one slug in three more or less dead on target. Dan Maffrey's visits got longer and longer. And then one afternoon round about sundown he began to talk, not just ordinary-like but very much to the point.

He started it off by saying, 'What're you aiming to do, Johnny, when we quit this place?'

Now I hadn't given the future much thought up till then so I went on cleaning the Colt and did a little plain and fancy thinking.

At last I looked up at him and said, 'I reckon I'll just go on riding North. Folks say there's a big future up in the northern territories, gold in Montana, cattle in Wyoming. Could be a man could find a place to settle down in.'

'It's a mighty good idea, Johnny.' Maffrey paused, then said, 'But there's a favour I'd ask of you before you get round to sitting down and punching cattle.'

'Why, sure, Dan,' I said. 'Anything you ask.'

'It's like this,' he said. 'While I've been lying in that shed for the past two weeks I've done a lot of thinking, especially about those former pardners of mine, Mitch Fenton, Abe Somers and Willamette.'

Now it may have been my imagination working over hard but as he said those three names a kind of shiver went through me. And at the same moment the bright sunlight was gone and the far-off ranges went blue. I knew then that I was back again in the kind of world I'd always known since the war ended. I was back on the dark trail leading nowhere, back among the ghost towns and the outlaw hideouts.

I looked up and there he was, tall and black against the orange western sky.

'Yes,' I said, a mite huskily.

'They're not going to get away with it,

Johnny. They took all I'd got, they shot me down and left me for dead. And now it's my turn. I'm going on their trail. I'm going to take all they've got and I'm going to shoot them down one by one, just as I would shoot down a pack of coyotes.'

He paused, and light faded out of the western sky and a small cold wind blew down from the high country. I shivered again.

Maffrey went on talking again but this time almost like a man talking to himself. 'They'll go down all right, but unlike me they're not going to live to tell their tale.' He stared down at me again. 'Not as long as I've got you with me, Johnny Ross.'

I sat there a brief space longer, thinking that this was how it was. There was a pattern in a man's life and you couldn't get away from it. You might struggle and cuss but the pattern was always there. There was a part to be played out to the bitter end. I felt I owed Maffrey something. I knew he'd been wronged. And yet I still boggled at the thought of the vengeance trail he was proposing to lead me on.

His voice came like a whisper of wind in the tall timber of the hills.

'We could do big things together, Johnny.'

And I thought yes, by grab, we could

35

indeed. I could see somewhere a long green valley dotted with grazing cattle and a white clapboarded ranchhouse with a rocker out on the porch and somewhere inside there was a figure, a woman's figure, not clear–

I said, 'OK., Dan, I'll take the trail with you.'

I stood up and he clasped my left hand with one of his not saying a word and we walked together back to the adobe in the darkness.

CHAPTER THREE

It took us several days to get onto the trail of the three Texans and before we finally struck it at Gillburg Crossing a number of things had happened.

We said adios to Jesus Garcia and his wife Maria. They insisted on giving us as much food as we could carry. They refused the little money we offered them and told us to go with God. We rode off then into the bright morning. Dan Maffrey riding tall in his saddle alongside of me. It all felt pretty good until I remembered what we were aiming to do. Maffrey had said no more about getting on the trail of the others but I knew that he had no other idea than that in his big handsome head and I had accepted it.

So we rode on through desert country with high barren mountains far off to our right. This was the only trail those three hombres could have taken and we just followed along still heading north. A day passed. We camped for the night in the lee of a ridge. We ate sparingly of the bread, beans and coffee

37

Jesus Garcia had given us and slept.

Next morning we rode on again, deeper now into the hills. We entered a brown-walled sand-floored canyon soon after midday and were ambling quietly along when we heard gunshots. Somewhere up the trail ahead of us.

I looked across at Dan Maffrey and he looked back at me.

'Trouble,' I said.

'We've got troubles of our own, Johnny.'

'Sure,' I said. 'Sure.'

'We'll cut back and circle round the hills,' he said.

We were just about to wheel our mounts around when I heard a scream. I looked up the canyon bed. A solitary rider was coming licketty-split towards us. About a couple of hundred yards behind going all out and yelling was a small band of Indians. Apaches, I thought. And then I shouted, 'Dan, it's a woman.'

We dismounted fast. Dan had unsheathed his Winchester and I had my Colt awkward in my left hand. She must have seen us and came rocking along straight at us. And then she was past in a cloud of dust and I heard Maffrey's rifle crash out beside me. They were still out of range of the Colt and then they got near. Near enough. Maffrey's gun roared again and I saw a horse and rider go down. I brought the Colt up then and when the nearest Apache was not more than ten yards off I let him have it plumb centre. He just threw up his arms and reeled backwards off his cayuse. I thought 'Good for you, hand' and targeted a second. He was mighty close by this time and the slug well nigh tore his head off.

The dust was all boiled up around us but through it I saw one more Apache and he was making off just about as fast as his pony could carry him. I wiped sweat drops off my nose and turned to look for the girl. She was standing by her horse with her head pressed into its neck. She wasn't very much to look at. Not from where I was anyways. She was wearing a blue cotton dress and her hair was a sort of lightish brown.

Dan Maffrey and I went up to her and she slowly turned her head round and looked at us. And now there was a whole lot to look at. She was prettier than anyone I ever did see, with a sort of oval face and fine eyebrows and big blue tear-filled eyes.

She stared at us for a long moment.

Then she kind of wailed, 'They're all dead, all of them.'

Thinking she meant the Indians and was still afraid, I said, 'Sure, ma'am. They're all dead or gone.'

'It's Ma an' Pa and Jimmy,' she cried.

Maffrey said grimly, 'We'd better go look. Maybe we aren't too late.'

We got her back on her pony and rode north up the canyon to the bend round which she'd come not more than five minutes before. And then in another mile we knew what she'd been talking about, and by God, it wasn't easy to look at.

Two burnt-out wagons lay overturned on the sand. Nearby lay three huddled shapes.

I said, 'You wait here with Dan, miss.' Then I went over and took a look. It wasn't the first time I'd seen Death's ugly face but it was uglier than ever. There were the usual mutilations that the goddam Apaches seem to enjoy. Standing there I wondered what it was all about. These folks had come hundreds of miles through freezing cold and baking heat. They'd gone without food, and clothes and every little comfort a human being longs for. And what waited for them at the end of the trail? Not ripening corn or yellow gold. No rocker on the porch. Nothing. Or just horror. The nightmare of a grinning Apache warrior, the heart-freezing horror of the axe and the knife.

I turned away from what was left of this little family and went back to where the girl and Dan Maffrey were standing quietly by the horses.

'There's work to be done,' I said, feeling kinda awkward in the presence of grief.

'If you'll take the horses, miss, and go over to that clump of trees, Dan and I will see to it.'

She nodded dumbly and went off with the horses. Dan and I went over to the wagons. We found a spade and dug a good big hole in the dry desert floor. Then we put the man, the woman and the boy in it and covered it well up and mounded it. We found some stones and rocks and set them in place over the fresh-dug sand and then I fashioned a cross out of two pieces of wood from a box that had escaped the fire.

Most of the day was gone by the time we'd finished our chore. Shadows lengthened out, dark purple over on the west side of the canyon. We tidied away the family possessions the Apaches had scattered about around the wagons and then Dan Maffrey went over to fetch the girl.

When they reached the graveside the sunlight was all gone and the canyon was grey and silent. Somewhere up on the mesa a coyote howled.

I said, 'Maybe you could say a few words, Dan.'

He didn't reply but slowly took off his big wide-brimmed hat. Then he slowly began to say the Lord's Prayer. We stood there hat-less, the only sound the sobbing of the girl standing between us. When Dan was done we walked away and left the girl kneeling by the grave of her family.

She came back to us about a quarter of an hour later. She was quiet and composed now, but her eyes looked empty of all interest. Maybe she was looking at some-thing we couldn't see, some picture in the mind's eye that shut her away from us both.

Maffrey said, 'Let's move on up canyon a way and then we'll camp for the night.'

It was dark now and I have never thought much of the belief still common in the South-West that Apaches won't attack in the dark. They'll attack and burn and kill at any old time is my idea and I figure it's better to be scared of Apaches than dead.

'Let's get onto higher ground,' I said. 'I'd kinda like to feel a wall at my back.'

So we moved on for a mile or so up canyon in thickening darkness until at last we found an angle in the wall with a big rock sticking out on the far side. We looked at it and figured it would do. We shared out our food and drank water instead of coffee. We didn't feel safe enough to light a fire.

I risked building a cigarette when we'd done eating and when I was lighting it I heard the girl speak, almost for the first time since she'd come screaming down the trail towards us.

For a time I didn't pay much attention to what she was saying. I was just listening to the sound of her voice, soft and low and gentle and then I gathered she was trying to thank us for what we'd done.

So after a bit as her voice tailed off I said, 'Shucks, ma'am. It's little enough.' And then I thought to ask her name.

'I'm Jeannie Bain,' she said, 'and I'm sure obligated to you both.'

There was something about the way she spoke that made me ask her where she and her folks had come from.

'Why, from South Carolina,' she said.

'Well,' I said, 'if that don't beat all. My Pa and Ma came from there too.'

Dan Maffrey who hadn't been saying much seemed interested in this.

'I come from Texas, ma'am,' he said.

'Yes,' she said, 'I guessed you were from there. They say all Texas men are big and tall.'

'Yes,' says Dan, 'reckon so. Texas is a mighty big country an' it needs big men to run it.'

Well, after that there wasn't much to say so we agreed to get some sleep. I said I'd keep watch for half the night and Dan Maffrey agreed to do the rest. I gave the girl my bed-roll and she thanked me. Then they lay down one on each side of the rock. I found myself another rock a little way out into the canyon and prepared to sit out the next five or six hours.

A man gets to thinking at times like these and I did a lot of thinking that night. All the past years started coming up before me like pictures on a magic lantern screen. We'd had a magic lantern back in the old days when I was a kid in South Caroliny and I remembered it well. It had been fun and then the War came and bust everything up. I'd learned to use a gun when I was fourteen. At fifteen the air was full of war talk and a year later in '61 the trouble between the North and the South began. It wasn't long before I was itching to have a crack at the goddam Yankees and in '63 I got into the army and had all the cracks I wanted. The first big one was at Chancellorsville and soon after that we went marching into the Shenandoah Valley. Then came Gettysburg and I was in the attack from the South. It was hell with the lid off all right – an unending blast of gunfire and men I knew died all round me screaming for God's mercy as their life blood poured out into the cornfields and hillsides.

An owl hooted twice up on the eastern side of the canyon and I listened carefully for an Apache to give the answering call but no call came, so I figured it was an owl after all. I went on listening for a while but there was nothing wrong out there so I went back to my magic lantern and the lean years just after the War.

I'd gone back to my old home but my Ma and Pa were old and tired and had nothing much to say to a young man fresh home from war. I stuck it for a year helping out on the farm but it wouldn't answer something a-calling inside me, something working like yeast. I was as restless as a young stallion and one day in the late fall of 1866 I packed a bag, saddled up the mare I'd bought, said goodbye to my folks and hit the trail south-west towards Texas. I could ride a horse and I'd learned how to use a gun, and I soon found that these were mighty useful accomplishments in Texas in 1866. I got in on one of the first cattle drives to be made after the War. Texas was swarming with long-horns in those days, lean, tough, dangerous critters and I got work helping round up thousands of wild unbranded cattle on a ranch about fifty miles south of San Antone. It all came back, as the past always does to me, in big pictures, great masses of the cattle bawling and milling on the flat just south of old John Walker's ranch. The drive up the trail in the Spring of '67, the flooded Red River and the cattle rolling their eyes as they swam across; a running fight with Kiowas in the Indian territory north of the river and Shorty Gunn being buried on the lone prairie he'd sung about so often when night-herding the cows.

And then Abilene. Abilene in 1868. The first and worst of the cow-towns. It roared all day and it roared all night. Fresh off the long trail we roamed the streets and kept the bartenders busy on a twenty-four hour bust. A lot of stupid things have been said and written about the cowboys who came to Abilene and later to Wichita and Dodge. Most of them had been through the war, most of them were young and wild. Shooting off a gun meant no more than rolling a smoke. The town was wide open. Saloons,

honky-tonks, sporting houses went up overnight and as the cattle rolled in the money
rolled in too.

I sniffed the night-air, mighty clean and
cool after the heat and stench of memory.
Everything was quiet. I pulled out my fob-
watch. I'd bought it from Keenan's Emporium in Abilene and it was still going. It was a
half-hour after midnight. A couple of hours
to go and I could get some sleep while Dan
Maffrey sat up with his memories whatever
they were.

Mine settled down again to the Abilene
days, the time when I danced with Dora
Hand came swimming up out of the dark
caves. Wild Bill Hickok had been there then,
in the Alamo, all dolled up in chequer-board
pants and a fancy waistcoat, his hair curled
and oily hanging over his shoulders and his
long moustaches giving him a pretty sour
look. That was the time he'd crossed over to
where I sat with Dora Hand and said, 'Get
going, son, I want to talk with this lady.' And
being young and knowing all about Wild Bill
and his derringers I'd moved off. I could
learn all I wanted to know from any one of
the other fairybelles as they came to be
known in the later and even wilder days at
Dodge. The lessons weren't cheap but they

were mighty interesting to a young heller of twenty. Sitting there in the dark I said to myself, 'a young heller of twenty', and now I was an older heller of thirty gone and nothing to show, nothing more than a busted-up hand, a hoss and a saddle and what was left of a hundred dollars I'd won in the poker game at Newtown from my ex-pals, the Owens boys.

And at that point I must have fallen asleep, for the next thing I remembered was Maffrey's voice saying:

'Wake up, Johnny, I'll take over till first light.'

I said, 'thanks,' rather guiltily. It had been plumb stupid of me to sleep like that when other folks were depending on me.

I went over to where the girl lay, wrapped myself in Maffrey's blanket and was off to sleep before you could say 'Lights out.'

I woke up just as the grey dawn lifted over the canyon. It was cold and my wounded hand ached. I stared around for a bit but there wasn't hide nor hair of a warrior to be seen. The girl, Jeannie, sat up, her eyes wild, and I said 'Good morning, miss' and she took me and the empty unfriendly morning in slow-like. The wild look went out of her eyes bit by bit and she began to weep.

48

I stood up and walked across to Dan Maffrey.

He said, 'I reckon we might risk a small fire and make some coffee.'

I said, 'The girl needs it even more than we do.'

So we collected some mesquite twigs and got a fire going and soon we were drinking hot black coffee and eating bacon and beans.

'If I'm not mistaken,' Dan Maffrey said, as he rolled himself a smoke, 'we're more than twenty miles south of Bentville. If we get going we'll make it before noon.'

'And then you'll be among decent folks again, miss,' I said.

'Yes,' she said in her soft quiet voice and then added, 'You're decent folks too. And I'm sure beholden to you both, even if you're not.'

'Well,' said Dan Maffrey. 'I figure we didn't do any more than any other men would do in the circumstances. So you needn't go on thanking us. We'll just move along to Bentville and see what we can find for you there.'

Well, the girl looked kind of sad but I didn't think any more about it at the time. We got busy rubbing out the fire and tending to the horses. Then just as sunlight began to light up the western top of the canyon wall we mounted and rode on north.

We kept our eyes skinned for Apaches, smoke signals and other signs of trouble but trouble didn't come. We just rode on and after an hour's riding we came out of the canyon onto flat desert again. But it wasn't to last long. Not two miles ahead of us the land rose steadily and soon we were way above the desert and riding slow through scrub-covered hills, with occasional thickets of live oak and clumps of mesquite and chaparral. It wasn't long before we struck a trail heading west and we figured we couldn't be far from Bentville.

It took another hour to get there and we saw it suddenly as we came round the bend of a valley. It wasn't much to look at. Just a main street with three or four saloons, a few stores and some shacks that looked as if they'd just been stuck down anywhere.

As we rode down the grade heading into the centre of the town I saw one man detach himself from a door post and disappear fast. The whole place looked empty, a ghost town just waiting to blow away.

He halted on the edge of town and stared uncertainly. The whole place looked uneasy,

50

uninviting, but there was nothing else to do other than ride on in and see what happened.

Dan Maffrey was the only one to speak. He had sat his horse staring silently at the empty street and then he said suddenly, 'We'll learn something about them here.'

I knew what he meant and as I got my cayuse moving I shivered, not really knowing why.

CHAPTER FOUR

We came to a halt right outside a two-storeyed frame building in the centre of the town. A large board hung askew from the railings above the entrance. It bore the name in large sun-faded letters 'California House'. In a window left of the batwing doors a yellowed notice showed the words 'Rooms to Let'.

We stood near the sagging hitch-rack, waiting, as if someone might come out and say, 'Welcome, folks'. But no one came out and no word was spoken until Dan Maffrey broke the silence.

'Reckon this'll do for the time being,' he said.

The girl, Jeannie, nodded her head warily. We all dismounted, unstrapped our bed-rolls and then walked into the hotel. The batwing doors gave straight into a large saloon. There was a long bar facing us and way over to our right a square cut staircase. Two men were sitting at a table immediately under the staircase. Behind the bar dozed a large fat man. As we stood hesitating in the doorway he opened one eye and stared at us.

It was kind of an invitation to speak up and say our piece. Dan walked over to the bar.

'You have some rooms to let, mister,' he said.

The bartender didn't speak for some time but I could see his one open eye glaring angrily at Dan.

'Could be,' was all he said after a long think.

'We could use two-three rooms,' Dan said, still soft and pleasant-like.

'How long?' said the man grudgingly.

'A coupla days,' said Dan.

This gave the bartender a lot of food for thought. I watched his eye roll over in the direction of the two men by the staircase. A fat pink tongue travelled slowly across his thick lower lip.

'No,' he said at last. 'Them rooms is all booked-up.'

Now this seemed to make Dan Maffrey about as mad as I was feeling. He leaned across the bar-top and grabbed himself a big fistful of the bartender's shirt. With this he heaved the man off his perch, banging him right up against the other side of the bar.

'Listen, mister,' he said, 'we're three tired and hungry travellers. We've been a-fighting Indians and that poor girl there has had her Ma and Pa and young brother killed before her eyes by a pack of murdering Apaches. We don't aim to travel any more so we'll have those two-three rooms you've got stashed away upstairs or I'll push a whisky bottle down your fat gullet.'

The barman's eye had popped wide-open by this time. The other eye hadn't, I realised, because it wasn't there.

'All right, all right,' he growled. 'You kin have the rooms.'

Dan released him and he went to a drawer and got three keys. He threw them down on the counter.

'That'll be two dollars a day each. One day in advance.' I dug into the old sock and paid him.

'Numbers three, five and six,' he growled again.

'Thanks,' said Dan. 'When's the next stage out of here?'

'Stage to Durango comes through here in two days' time.' Words came out of him like gold coins from a miser's hoard.

'We can put you on that, Miss Jeannie,'

55

said Dan to the girl. 'From there you can get back East to your folks, easy-like.'

'I've got no folks now,' said the girl.

'We'll think of something. Don't fret yourself.' He looked over at me.

'Let's go look at these rooms, Johnny.'

I said to the bartender, 'Where do our horses sleep?'

He said, 'There's a barn in back. I'll put 'em in there.'

We went on upstairs then. The three men in the saloon followed our progress until we were out of sight.

'This seems a queer sort of town,' I said as we reached the upper landing.

'Yes,' agreed Dan Maffrey. 'There's something peculiar going on hereabouts and I figure they're not overly anxious to have strangers poking and prying about.'

We located our three rooms so grudgingly let. They weren't exactly de luxe as you might say, but each of them had a bed in it which was something. We gave the girl the one that looked cleanest and arranged to meet downstairs in fifteen minutes to see if we could get some chuck.

There was a basin and ewer on a washstand in my room and as I washed up I could feel my empty belly banging about against my ribs like a starving tiger in a cage. I had another look at my money before putting on my vest again. There were eight-eighty dollars left, enough I figured to buy what we wanted and pay the girl's fare back East. The future, like the past, would have to look after itself.

I was downstairs in the saloon before the others so took it on myself to do some ordering.

The bartender was standing up this time and making a show of polishing a glass with a bright pink cloth. I noticed that his suspenders were pink too.

I tried a smooth approach.

'How difficult would it be for you to cook us up some chuck, friend?'

He stopped polishing the glass and glared at me with his one eye for a long spell.

'This ain't an eating-house, mister,' he said surlily.

'It's a hotel, ain't it?'

He chewed that one over for another long minute.

'I've got this bar to look after, mister. I can't tend bar, clean this saloon and cook on top of it.' A faint whining note had crept into his voice I noticed so I pressed home my point.

'Shucks!' I said, 'I bet you could cook us up something if you just tried. Tell you what, friend. I'll tend bar while you go and wield the fry-pan.'

Again he seemed lost in ponderous unwilling thought. He threw a glance over at the two men at the table and one of them nodded. At last he said grudgingly, 'All right, mister. But I don't guarantee that what I cook will be fit to eat.'

I said, 'Fine, we'll take a chance on that.'

He went out through a door next to the bar and I went round behind it.

I could hear him banging tins and pans about, inside, venting his bad temper on the cooking utensils. But something else was cooking apart from what the bartender was hoping to poison us with. And I aimed to find out.

'Belly up to the bar, gents,' I called out cheerfully. 'Drinks are on the house.'

Now this seemed to rouse the two men who had been sitting all this while over by the staircase. I saw the bigger of the two jerk his head in my direction and then they both got up and ambled over towards the bar.

Spending time on the trail and moving about among all kinds of folk a man can get to know other men pretty well. You get to know the good and the half-good and the half-bad and the real bad. And the two hombres coming towards me now fitted as snug as two bugs in a rug into division number four. They looked as mean and ornery as you could hope to meet.

'What'll it be?' I said, as they drew up to the bar.

'Whisky,' said the tall one. He had a face like something carved carelessly out of a chunk of stone. The only moving thing in it were his eyes, small, black, mean and crafty.

'Yessir,' said his friend. He was smaller than the other man, and his face was round and doughy-looking, very pale for a man of his kind. His eyes were the same brand as the other's but more calculating, more deadly. A drooping, frontiersman's moustache made you notice his pale skin and gave him a general air of misery.

I found a bottle of Old Crow behind the bar and I planked this down together with three shot glasses. There seemed to be time for a little sociability before the shooting began. I filled the three glasses. I raised mine and gave them what's known on the back trails as the outlaw's toast. They both stared hard at me and then they both drank too.

I rolled a cigarette and felt their eyes boring into my poor old right hand.

'You got yourself a bad hand there, mister,' said the taller of the two.

I licked the cigarette paper, stuck it down, and said, 'Yes, but my left more than makes up for it.'

And then there were footsteps on the staircase. It was Dan Maffrey and Jeannie coming down. We all stared at her. And no wonder. She'd done something with her hair and her dress and looked as pretty as all get out.

Dan didn't bring her over to the bar as you might expect. He just took her over to a table on the right of the bar and sat her down there. Then he sat down and they waited then just like a lady and gent in a fashionable eating-house in some big Eastern city. I'd never seen one but I figured that Dan Maffrey had and knew exactly what to do there.

I sang out, 'You folks want a drink?'

I saw Dan Maffrey lean forward and say something to Jeannie and then he called back, 'We'll eat first, Johnny. Time for a drink afterwards.'

I turned my attention back to the two men at the bar.

60

'How about another one?' I said.

'Suits us fine,' said the short man throatily.

I filled the glasses again and we drank, without the outlaw's toast this time.

There was a pretty good smell coming from the kitchen now. It made me feel I could eat a steer, horns, hide and all.

Then old One-Eye the bartender came in with a tray and three plates of steaming food, so I skipped out from behind the bar and went over to Dan and Jeannie. If I could only hold off trouble for just so long as it would take to get this chuck under my belt all would be well.

We ate hungrily and when we'd finished the hash and potatoes, the barman brought us some apple-pie and coffee. Not with any good grace but still he brought it and we three tucked it away, Jeannie with as much of an appetite as Dan or me. The two men who had been at the bar had now gone back to their table.

'Sure is good,' said Jeannie at last with a kind of satisfied sigh.

'Yes,' I said. 'Sure is.' But my attention was wandering. Two more rough-looking hombres in soiled range clothes had batted open the saloon swing doors and came now swaggering over to the bar.

61

They could have been a couple of hands from some neighbouring cattle outfit or drovers from some trail herd. But somehow I didn't figure they were. There weren't any ranches so far as I knew in this part of the territory, and trail herds usually kept to the Chisholm trail many miles east of where we were sitting.

I leaned forward across the table.

'I reckon there's trouble brewing,' I mumbled.

'In that case, Johnny, I think we'd better send Miss Jeannie here to bed.'

I looked at the girl. She'd turned pale at my words and one pretty hand had crept up towards her throat.

'Please,' she whispered. 'Please don't get into trouble, especially on my account.'

'It isn't you they're after, Miss Jeannie,' I said, 'It's us.'

'We'll just escort you over to the stairs,' said Dan. 'Then you can go on up to bed and get some rest. No call to worry over us, miss. We can look after ourselves, can't we, Johnny?'

'You're tooting,' I said and stood up, giving myself a good clear view of the room as I did so. But they weren't ready for any hanky-panky yet and we took the girl over to the staircase without anything more than a couple of looks from the two newcomers at the bar.

On the first stair the girl stopped, and turning said, 'Good night.'

We both said 'Good night.' Then when she had gone Dan Maffrey began to walk towards the bar.

'Reckon we'll have that drink you were talking about,' he said.

'Two whiskies,' I said, looking at the bartender.

The two newcomers now gave us their attention.

'You heading for Gillburg, gents?' said the nearer one.

'Could be,' said Dan friendly-like. 'You from there?'

'It's our little home from home,' said the other man with a sort of guffaw. 'Ain't it, Sam?'

'That's right,' said Sam. 'A little home from home.' And he too gave a short hard bark of laughter.

Dan gave them a long cool sort of look.

Then he said slow-like, 'The name Mitch Fenton mean anything to you? Or mebbe you would have heard of Abe Somers or a hombre called Willamette?'

Now both these had played poker, probably in their cradles, if they ever had cradles, which I doubted. But neither of them could quite prevent that little look in the eye which is always there when you ask a man if he knows someone that he does know, if you understand me. And, looking at these two, both Dan Maffrey and I knew that they knew not only Mitch Fenton, but Abe Somers and Willamette too. I saw Dan's face go cold and set. And a spot between my shoulder blades began to itch, always a sure sign of trouble to me. So I said quick-like, 'How about a hand of poker?'

The question broke the ice that was beginning to form on our little puddle.

The man called Sam said, 'Suits me,' and his pardner nodded agreement. But they both looked as cagey as a couple of cats near a dog.

'Lend us a deck of cards, One-Eye,' said Sam to the bartender.

So One-Eye was his name as I might have known and they knew him too. Just as they knew Mitch Fenton and Company. The whole thing was getting to be more and more interesting.

One-Eye handed over a new deck of cards.

'Feel like a game?' Sam called out to the

two over at the table.

'Why not?' The rock-faced man got up and walked heavily over towards us. I noticed he was wearing two guns, both tied down in holsters to his upper legs. His friend followed him.

We moved in a body then to the larger table where not long before Jeannie and Dan and I had eaten our meal. The bartender came round and cleared off the dishes and we all sat down. One-Eye came back with drinks and we settled down with something more than just the usual small excitement a man feels when about to be engaged in a battle of wits.

I decided it ought to be a social kind of affair. I sure like to know the name of a gent I'm going to play cards with and I'm even more insistent about the name of a gent I have to kill. Both possibilities lay before me so I spoke up before the man holding the cards got down to any serious work.

'My name's Johnny Ross,' I said, nice and conversational-like.

A man would have thought I'd said 'Jesse James' or 'Emperor Napoleon'. They just sat there and goggled a bit. However, the man called Sam recovered fairly quick.

'My name's Sam Billings and this hyar

hombre' – he jerked a dirty thumb in the general direction of his pardner – 'he's Noisy Nate to his friends.'

I looked enquiringly across at the rock-faced one who'd been sitting at the table with his pardner. He caught my look and threw it back at me.

'Name's no matter,' he said in a peculiar grating voice. His mean little eyes roved carefully across my features.

Dan Maffrey then tossed his name into the pool and they all sat staring at him as if to make certain of knowing him for a long time to come. Sam Billings broke the silence finally by starting to deal. There was more silence then while we concentrated on our cards. Mine were no song and dance act so I passed, and then the game finally settled down to a duel between Dan Maffrey and Sam Billings. At last Dan called his opponent who laid down two pairs but Dan raked in the pot with a full house.

Rock-face who wouldn't give his name dealt and I saw him give his pal a small look across the table so I thought: Right, you low-down sons, I'm a-waiting. Very quiet-like I eased the Colt with my left hand and took a look at Dan. He saw it and gave a small imperceptible nod.

This round my hand was good – good enough for a big kill, I played for time leading off with a dollar in the pot. Sam Billings raised me. Dan passed and Noisy Nate drew a card. Rock-face passed but his friend put five in which left things open for me. In I went again with ten dollars. This seemed to excite Sam Billings and he raised me again.

I took a good look at my cards. Four fine queens. Bigger I reckoned than the threes or straight old Massa Billings was probably bluffing on.

'Thirty bucks says I win.' I peeled them off my dwindling roll and pushed them into the centre of the table.

I laid out my four fair queens in a neat row, and kept my eye on Rock-face. His right hand was sliding slowly, almost imperceptibly, off the table edge.

Sam Billings flung down a nine, ten and jack of clubs. His face was working. The queen of hearts followed on top of the jack and then the king.

'A goddam crooked game,' he yelled and reached for his gun. Even as I wondered who'd popped the extra queen in I pushed the table over into his lap and into Rock-face's lap as well. My Colt came out faster than it had done since I started practice. Some other gun exploded down on the floor. Somewhere over on my right a big figure was standing and suddenly his gun went into action. Over the terrific detonations there was one high cry followed almost immediately by a horrifying sort of strangled grunt.

I held my gun on Rock-face's pal who seemed more dangerous than Noisy Nate. There was a loud kind of silence after the racket of gunfire and gunsmoke drifted in grey veils in the lamplight.

'A put-up job, friend?' Dan Maffrey moved over towards the man I was covering.

The only reply was a kind of snarl. Dan raked his gun-barrel against the side of the man's face and he too went down. Watching Dan I could see rage working in him like yeast. He turned on Noisy Nate, swinging his gun up as he did so.

'No, not me,' mumbled Nate. 'I wasn't in on it. I ain't drawn. Look.' And he held up both hands high to show how harmless he was.

'In on what?' Dan's voice was cold like winter ice.

'Nothin'. It was just a manner of speakin'.' Nate trembled where he stood.

'I'll count up to three, mister,' said Dan.

'If by then you haven't said what they were in on I'll shoot you in the stomach.'

'No! No!' The words seemed to be wrenched from the shivering centre of Nate's miserable little being.

'One,' said Dan Maffrey.

'They'll kill me if I tell.'

'Who'll kill you, mister, if I don't? Two.'

'The gang. The gang,' yelled Nate. 'We was sent down from Gilburg Crossing – just in case. Mitch figured that even if one of you was dead the other would be coming up the trail after him. I didn't ask to be in on it. I shore didn't.'

I looked at Dan Maffrey and was scared of what I saw. His eyes had a mighty strange glazed look.

I butted in fast. There were enough bodies lying around for the time being.

'You mosey on out of here fast, friend Nate,' I said. 'Get on back to Gilburg Crossing and tell your pardners that we're coming after them fast.'

'I'll tell 'em. I'll tell 'em,' gabbled Nate.

'You'd better tell 'em that their gun-slinging friends are dead too,' added Dan.

I holstered my Colt and heaved the table back into position. Dan Maffrey was right but I gasped at what I saw. Sam Billings and

Rock-face were dead all right but what made me shiver was that they were both drilled between the eyes and the two pair of eyes were open and surprised-like as though they couldn't quite believe it had happened to them.

Rock-face's friend began to come round then with a good deal of moaning and groaning. Very slowly he hoisted himself into a sitting position, from where he surveyed his two dead friends slowly and incredulously. Then he looked up at us shaking his head.

'Can't believe it. Can't believe it. He was the fastest gun in the whole territory.'

'Who was?' I said.

'Why Pike Maun, of course, who else?' He groaned and put a hand up to his red swollen cheekbone.

'Well,' I said, 'he's met his match so you and your friend here can tote him and Sam Billings out of here just about as fast as you like.'

He got up slow and painful-like and he and Noisy Nate between them took away the remains.

Dan Maffrey said, 'We'll stay a night and then push on to Gilburg Crossing. I don't aim to stay here and be drygulched before

70

the stage comes. We'll find another stage for the girl there.'

'Yes,' I said. There wasn't much else to say.

I became aware of the bartender watching us.

'Sam Billings or the other one, Pike Maun, drew first, remember,' I said.

'Yes, sir,' he said and winked his one eye in a hideous gesture of agreement. 'That's how it was.'

And so we were left to get a night's sleep at the California House. I put my gun under my pillow and an uneasy sleep I had, unrefreshing, dream-troubled. Something was wrong with the pattern, something that didn't fit, but I couldn't put my finger on it.

CHAPTER FIVE

Next morning we were all up with the lark, except that there aren't any larks around Bentville. The bartender was up too, looking even more morose than he had the evening before, but still scared I figure because he hastened to assure us that our horses had been fed and watered. He got us some breakfast and stood watching us eat.

'You folks aimin' to stay here another day?' he asked at last.

'No,' said Dan coldly. 'We aren't. Just as soon as we've eaten we're going to ride on to Gilburg Crossing.'

'I thought you wanted to wait for the stage,' said the bartender.

'We did,' agreed Dan. 'But not now. This town's no place for a lady. Does a stage line run out of Gilburg?'

'There's an eastbound coach once a week.'

'That'll suit us, won't it, Miz Bain?' I said.

'I suppose so,' was all her answer, spoken with very little enthusiasm.

'How far is it?' I said to the bartender.

'Ten-hour ride from here, north.'

'Fine,' said Dan and pushed his chair back. 'Time to ride.'

We got up. I paid the bartender for our meals out of the winnings of the previous night's poker game. Then I went out, collected our three horses from the barn in the back of the hotel where they'd spent the night and brought them round to the front.

Jeannie and Dan were waiting. They mounted and we rode north out of Bentville. About a hundred yards from the hotel I turned in the saddle and looked back. The bartender was standing quite still on the porch of the California House watching us ride away. I wondered for a time what his part had been and then I dismissed him from my thoughts and settled down to the long ride ahead of us.

It was easy riding most of the way, with a climb up at first onto a great flat tableland, with two beehive shaped buttes over to the east of us. It was still early morning with the sun shining nicely, as soft and fine as frog's hair. I felt like singing and wondered why. Maybe it was being with these other folk. Jeannie, who although mighty quiet and lady-like, was mighty pretty too. And Dan Maffrey too. There were moments when I

74

just couldn't figure him at all. Last night's poker game and its grand finale was a case in fact. But other times he was a really affable feller, with a nice courteous way of treating folks that sure hit the spot. Yes, everything felt fine on that lovely morning so I sang a verse or two of a song I'd learned way down the Texas trail all about a gent who is walking in a street in Laredo and how he finds a poor cowboy lying in the mud, shot in the breast, and how the cowboy asks the gent,

> To beat the drum slowly and play the fife
>   lowly
> Play the dead march as you carry me along
> Take me to the green valley, there lay the
>   sod o'er me
> For I'm a young cowboy and I know I've
>   done wrong.

Well, as my voice tailed off and just as I was thinking what a real fine song it was for the morning air, Miss Jeannie looks across at me and says:

'That's a very sad song you've just been singing, Mr Ross. Don't you know any happy songs?'

So I said, 'Well, Miz Jeannie, I guess I just hadn't thought about it thataway.' I scratched

75

my head and tried to think of a cheerful little song, but the only ones that would come into my mind were more or less about the same sort of subject as the one I started with. There was one about a dying cowboy who didn't want to be buried on the lone prairie, and another about a puncher who says goodbye to his horse and a lot more and nearly all of them, come to think of it, were about death and dying and saying goodbye.

I said, 'Nope, Miz Jeannie. Reckon all the songs I know are a mite sad. Maybe if I go on thinking long enough I can dig up a happy one.'

'I hope so,' she said, kind of brisk. 'It's no good spending one's life thinking about death. We've got to make the most of life.' She looked at Dan riding just on her right. 'Don't you agree, Mr Maffrey?'

He gave her a long hard look.

'Yes,' he said at last. 'I suppose so. But to some of us death's a pretty important matter and now and then we have to give it a thought.'

Well that seemed to puzzle Miss Jeannie but I knew what he had in his mind. He was thinking of the two men he'd killed the night before and maybe of the other men, Mitch Fenton and Abe Somers and Willamette

76

who he'd try to kill some fine day or other.

Anyway I didn't sing any more songs. The big open tableland began to dip down and we were riding first downgrade and then upgrade again through a long rising valley with big hills on each side of us and what looked like a pass about a half-mile or so ahead. A small stream ran down on our left.

Dan Maffrey reined in when we were about half-way up the trail to the pass.

'I guess we could do with a breather just as much as the horses,' he said. So we climbed down. I looked at my old fob watch that I kept in the left-hand pocket of my vest. It was almost high noon.

'Time for chuck,' I said when I'd watered the horses, and the other two agreed.

We made ourselves comfortable in the shade of a clump of live oak and opened up a tin of beans. We ate these and some cold bacon that One-Eye the bartender had sold us, along with tobacco and a sack of oats for the horses. Jeannie Bain was recovering fast from the shock of the Apache raid and was now beginning to smile, kind of shy at first but really waking up and coming to life like a flower in the sun.

'How come your right hand's like that, Mr Ross?' she asked when she saw me rolling a smoke a mite awkwardly.

Well this was a dead-ringer all right. I just naturally didn't want to uncover my shameful past right there in front of such a nice girl.

'It was a mountain lion, Miz Jeannie,' I lied brazenly. 'It had toothache so I offered to draw the tooth. But it didn't take kindly to my offer and tried to chew my hand off.'

I tried to look her in the eye as I said all this, but her eyes as I said it got so cold and scornful that I just had to look somewhere else.

'I suspect that you are telling me a lie, Mr Ross,' she said. 'But it is for me to apologise. I ought not to have pried into other folk's private lives.'

She then turned to Dan who was grinning to himself and made herself very agreeable to him. And I was left to finish off my cigarette which I did so plumb clumsily that the whole thing fell to bits in my hands and I just threw it away.

And then just as I was glooming a bit over the past and present a shot came with a whine and a whiplash right between the three of us. Jeannie screamed.

I called out, 'Down an' make for cover.'

I only had the roughest kind of idea where that bullet came from but I waved the other two over to the shady side of the trail where there was a kind of dip in the ground. And down into this we slid. The second shot came just as we got there and this time I was watching. I saw the glint of a rifle barrel way up on the hillside west of the pass.

'I need my rifle,' said Dan. 'A Colt's no use at this range.'

'Risky to try for it,' I said. 'Howsomever I'm a smaller target than you, Dan, so I'll just see if I can crawl across to your hoss and get it.'

He mumbled something and I said, 'Never-no-mind,' and edged out of the hole backwards. It was almost twenty yards across to where the horses were picketed and I began to belly-crawl across the open space, trying to look like a worm on urgent business. The man on the ridge put a bullet not more than two yards from where I was inching along. Dust flew up and against my sweating face – it was that close. I crawled on, knowing now that if the next one didn't get me I would up and run for it. I stopped suddenly and the ruse worked. The next shot was short and two yards away at least. I leapt up and ran. Another shot helped me on my way but he had failed to get me.

I hurriedly dragged Dan Maffrey's rifle from the saddle scabbard. I opened the breach. It was fully loaded. It was a pity about my right hand. I couldn't even crook a finger round the trigger and you need two hands anyways for a Winchester '73. No, it was back over the open trail again. So I did it a bit differently. This time I just ran, giving our drygulching friend time enough for only one shot which, like something in a poem my Ma read to me long ago, just wasted its sweetness on the desert air. Then I was back in the hole and passing the rifle to Dan.

'He's up on the ridge west of the pass,' I said.

'Yes,' said Dan, 'I know,' and he began to lay his bullets careful-like around the spot where the shots had been coming from. He fired four times and there was one answering shot from the ridge and then silence.

'Keep him busy, Dan,' I said. 'I'll work around to him from the east.'

Jeannie suddenly piped up, 'No, Johnny Ross. There's no call for you to be risking your life.'

'No,' I said, getting out of the hole again in the same way as before. The words were like music in my ears but I went on just the same. As I moved away I heard Dan fire his Winchester again and then there was lots more silence, broken only by the crash and thunder of my progress, now on all fours, past mesquite bushes and rocks. Slowly I worked my way away from the trail and then north to a point east of where the ambusher was stashed away. It was slow going but at last I was close up above the pass and looking across it to the rise on the far side.

And then I saw him and his horse too, the latter well back from the ledge on which this hombre was lying with his rifle. I aimed to get round behind him and let him have it. I skipped over the ground fast now that I was well behind him. As I ran across the flat bed I drew my Colt and then quite suddenly we were bang up against each other. It was Noisy Nate, Sam Billings' pardner. While I had been fully hidden from him he must have decided to quit. He was already in the saddle as I came forward. He saw me and pulled his gun but my sudden appearance spooked the cayuse. It went up on its hind legs and then came down quick and ran like a bat out of hell almost straight for me. I dodged, tripped over a trailing root and went down with a whump that knocked the breath out of me. A gun crashed and then he was gone. I scrambled up but he was well out of range by this time. I just stood there a moment. I pushed back my Stetson and scratched the front of my head. They sure were mighty anxious to stop us getting to Gilburg Crossing.

I hurried down the hillside to where Jeannie and Dan were waiting. I told them what had happened and they were almost as puzzled as I was.

Dan said, 'I figure they know we're on their trail and they sure intend to stop us before we get too far.'

'Who are they?' said Jeannie.

'Well,' said Dan, 'it's quite a long story but I guess you'll have to know what all this shooting's about sooner or later, so we'd better make it sooner. Let's take the weight off our feet for a spell and I'll tell you all about it.'

So we all sat down and I rolled a cigarette while Dan told her the story about Mitch Fenton, Abe Somers and Willamette and how they'd attacked him, robbed him and left him for dead way back in the desert country. He told it slow and careful and cold, and as he talked I could see that it was about the only thing that really occupied his mind.

'And if it hadn't been for Johnny here there wouldn't be any story to tell,' he wound up.

For a time she sat quite silent, twisting a small gold ring round and round her middle finger.

'What are you aimin' to do, Mr Maffrey?'

she said at last, still playing with the ring and not looking at him.

'I'm going to make 'em pay,' said Dan.

'How?'

'Why, with their life's blood,' he said in his flat quiet way. She had looked up at that moment and I saw her eyes suddenly widen. It was chiefly horror, I guess, that caused it but there was a margin of something else too, a sort of fascination. Dan Maffrey seemed to have that kind of effect on folks.

She spoke up, however, with a directness we were beginning to find in all she said. 'They that take the sword shall perish by the sword,' she said with all the severity of a fire-eating preacher. 'You ought to be ashamed of such sentiments, Mr Maffrey. Vengeance is not yours.' She gave him a long look. 'I shall make it my business to persuade you against it.' And you could see from the look in her eye that it was the kind of thing she would probably enjoy doing, especially as it would keep her in the company of Mr Dan Maffrey.

'It's about ten mile to go from here to Gilburg Crossing,' I said. 'I figure we'd better arrive there after dark. It might be safer.'

'Yes,' said Dan, and then looking at Jeannie he went on, 'there's no call for you to worry, Miz Jeannie. We don't aim to do anything that will put you in any kind of danger. We'll get you on the eastbound coach before we attend to our own business.'

'Thank you,' she said, very prim and proper. 'But I'm not really afraid of things, you know.'

'Right,' said Dan. 'Let's ride.'

So we climbed into the saddle once more and rode cagily up to the pass.

There was no man with a gun waiting this time and we rode on through and then over to the edge where the country fell away beneath us down to the beginning of a huge empty stretch of flat yellow desert. It all lay there in the quiet afternoon light ready and waiting for folk to come and live in it and make it blossom.

Somewhere over to our left in the folds and curves of the hills would be Gilburg Crossing. So following the rough trail down from the pass we headed towards it. We rode for about two hours keeping our eyes peeled all the way for possible ambushes. But everything was as peaceful as Sunday-go-to-meeting.

We first saw the town as we came out of a small canyon. It lay on a flat stretch of benchland about a mile from where we were. For a time we just sat looking at it, and

I remember thinking that it must mean something quite different for each one of us.

'We'd be asking for trouble if we ride into town in a bunch,' I said. 'I reckon we'd do well to split up.'

Dan Maffrey, staring at the fair-sized huddle of houses on the benchland, nodded.

'Yes, I'll ride in from the east. You and Jeannie circle the town and come in from the north.'

'She might be safer with you, Dan,' I suggested.

'No, Johnny,' he pulled his gaze away from the town. 'I'll play this hand alone. It's me they'll be looking for.'

I muttered some kind of assent.

'Look for a quiet boarding-house for Jeannie,' he went on. 'Then when she's looked after come on in. You'll find me in the biggest saloon in town.'

We swung our horses' heads westward. Dan called out, 'So long.'

He rode leisurely away in the opposite direction.

For several minutes Jeannie sat there just gazing after him. Then at last she sort of sighed and said,

'I sure feel mighty obligated to Mr Maffrey. There's not many men who'd do all he's done for me.'

'All he's done and anything else besides, Miz Jeannie, is only what ought to be done,' I said. 'Now I figure we'd better get going or Dan Maffrey will be kept waiting and from what I know Gilburg Crossing's not the kind of place to wait about in.'

With that I tickled my cayuse with a spur and we trotted off over a ridge and way over to the far side of the town. The whole western sky blazed up in red and orange as we rode. Then slowly it paled and colour began to flow off the hills into a soft twilight. It was all mighty fine to look at and looking across at the town in which lamplights even now were beginning to twinkle I couldn't help wishing it was just an ordinary town into which we could ride and feel safe and at home.

But that wasn't to be, not apparently for folks like Dan Maffrey and me. Slowly we began to draw round north-west of the town and I edged the horses inward until at last I judged we would be about opposite the direction from which Dan would come.

About a quarter of a mile from the nearest buildings we crossed a rough bridge over a creek.

'Probably what gave the town its name,' I said to Jeannie.

'What are you going to do about me, Johnny?' The question came suddenly as most of her questions did.

'Well,' I said, 'the general idea is to ship you back East to where you came from, Miz Jeannie, on the first stage out of town.'

'It won't help,' she half-whispered. 'There's no one to go back to.'

'We're nearly there,' I said. 'We'll talk about it later.'

We were now close to the nearest houses, mostly shacks from what I could see. A dog in the last glimmer of light heard us and barked wildly. We rode on into a rough rutted street. Larger houses of the clapboard kind lined it.

'We'll need to ask, I reckon.' I was beginning to feel a bit lost.

Then I saw what looked like a livery stable and barn. A man was hanging a kerosene lamp from a nail on one of the doors.

We rode on up to the entrance.

'You got board and lodging for a couple of tired hosses,' I called out.

'That's what this place is for, mister,' said the man.

I climbed out of the saddle gladly and went round to help Jeannie down.

The livery stable keeper eyed us curiously.

'That'll be a dollar a night,' he said flatly.

I groped for a coin, found it and flipped it at him. He caught it with the skill of a man who considers money important.

'Maybe that would also pay for a little friendly help,' I said.

'Try me,' said the livery keeper.

'We're looking for a quiet respectable boarding-house for this young lady.'

'Then you ain't got far to look,' he said. 'There's only one respectable place in the whole town and that's Ma Tompkins' house just across the way.' He gestured vaguely at a half-seen frame house further down the street. There was a light I noticed in one of the upper windows. 'Respectable but it ain't often quiet, not in Gilburg Crossing – what with miners in on the spree an' trail-hands a-shoutin' for women and whisky.' As if to underline his words, a gun crashed out twice from further into town.

A look that could have been fear flitted like a shadow over the liveryman's face. I turned to the horses and removed our bedrolls.

'Come on, Miz Bain,' I said. 'Let's see what Ma Tomkins has to offer.'

And we started out across the street followed by the still curious eyes of the liveryman.

CHAPTER SIX

Ma Tompkins' house was four square, clapboarded and white. We went up to the porch on which there was a rocker. I stepped forward and knocked. We waited. At last there was a sound of footsteps, a short rattle of a chain and the door opened about six inches.

'Who's there?' said a female voice.

'Two weary travellers, ma'am,' I said. 'We're looking for accommodation.'

It sounded mighty good but there was a long suspicious silence.

'How'm I to know you're respectable folks?'

'I sure don't know,' I said. 'You'll just have to take our word for it.'

'So long as you don't come here from that evil man up at the Marshal's office maybe I kin do something,' she grumbled. There was another rattle of chain. 'And don't try any hanky-panky just because I'm opening this door. I've got a double-bar'l gun here and I'll sure fill your belly full of lead if you try anything.'

The door opened slowly, revealing a short fat woman clutching a large shotgun. She peered out at us over the barrel of the gun.

'Is that a girl?' she said.

'Yes, ma'am,' said Jeannie. 'I'd sure be grateful if you could let me have a room.' As she spoke she swayed forward and would have fallen if I hadn't grabbed her.

'She's plumb wore out,' I said.

'Bring her upstairs,' the fat woman said. 'There's a room just at the top she can have.'

Slowly we got upstairs followed by Ma Tompkins, as I assumed her to be. It was a good clean room with a handsome brass bedstead and lace curtains.

'Now if you git on out of here, young man, and leave everything to me,' said Ma Tompkins. 'What this young woman wants is some decent food an' a good night's rest.'

'Yes'm,' I said. I looked across at Jeannie. She sure was pale and tuckered out. 'Good night, Miz Jeannie, I'll come a-calling on you in the morning.'

'Yes,' she said, 'good night and take care of yourself and Mr Maffrey too.'

Somehow I didn't want to go but I edged out and went downstairs into the street and what lay at the end of it.

I didn't have far to go. There was a corner

just ahead of me and as I turned it the whole street suddenly flowered into bright and noisy life. Most of it, it's true, was half shut in behind the batwing doors of a dozen saloons and honkytonks that showed on both sides of the wide street. Somewhere ahead a pianist was strumming out a lively tune and standing there on the edge of it all I felt the same old excitement in my vitals that I'd felt a hundred times before in some wide-open town or other. A man comes in off the trail or down from the high country and the feeling grabs him and off he goes on a real old bender.

And then I remembered Dan Maffrey and his plans and a whole lot of excitement just drained out of me. I'd got to find him and then together we'd got to get on the trail of Mitch Fenton and Company which meant a lot of grief for all concerned and no time at all for wine, women and song. So I pursued my way, now onto a boardwalk where I saw two stores, one called Sloan's Emporium, the other Michael's Dry Goods. After this there was a small quiet-looking saloon called 'The Bonanza' and then just before the main intersection there was a barber-shop called Bucky's Tonsorial Parlour. There was a man sitting in the chair and the barber was just wiping the last bit of lather off the customer's face. I almost poked my nose through the window pane with excitement for the customer was my old friend, Abc Somers, just a-sitting there, his eyes closed like a sinister cherub basking in the soothing ministrations of Bucky, the tonsorial artist.

I drew away from the window fast. This was no time for greetings. I looked around for the largest saloon I could see for that was where Dan Maffrey had said he would be. There was one right next to the barber shop – Miner's Rest, but although bright and noisy it couldn't compare with another one just a little further up the street – big and garish, the name Palace lit up with two flaming naptha lights. Light streamed from the windows and music tinkled out. This, I thought, would be the place. I began to move along the street. A drunk rolled out of the batwing doors and caromed off one of the pillars supporting the ornamental first floor balcony. He swore angrily and roamed off blindly into the dark alley running down to the right of the saloon. I moved on and mounted the boardwalk. A group of ponies stood restlessly at the tie-rail. I couldn't see Dan Maffrey's horse but that didn't mean a thing. I went up to the batwing doors and pushed my way in.

The bar-room was large and high and full of a thin fog of tobacco-smoke. The bar was long and lined with thirsty hombres and the blackjack, faro and poker tables were crowded. I sidled in right of the doors avoiding attention and stopped to get a clear picture of the place. When the pattern of trouble begins to take shape a man's got to be quite clear in his mind about such things as doors and windows, staircases and balconies. Also what kind of lights might have to be shot out. This last, I thought, my eyes roving carefully over the mob of drinkers and gamblers, would be hard work for a whole platoon of sharpshooters. There were lights everywhere, hanging in twinkling chandeliers over the tables or singly above the huge mirror behind the bar. Someone had spent a lot of money furnishing up the Palace.

And then I saw Dan Maffrey. He was standing down at the far end of the long bar, with his Stetson pushed well back off his forehead and looking as if he hadn't a care in the wide world. I edged my way towards him through the knots of card-players. No one took any notice of me in the noise and smoke and I was soon standing just next to him, and he just said 'Howdy' as though this was the most natural place for the two of us to be.

There was just enough room for me to squeeze in between Dan and a husky, bearded miner in a blue check shirt. A trio of bartenders were scuttling around filling orders but I managed to catch the eye of one of them and he came over.

'Whisky,' I said.

He was a sad-looking individual with a ripe red nose. But he brought a bottle and a glass and filled Dan's and then mine. I paid him with a silver dollar. Then I raised my glass.

'To the future,' I said. 'Abe Somers is in town. In the barber-shop.'

'The future,' echoed Dan, looking mighty grim and purposeful.

I put my glass down, turned my back to the bar and began to roll a cigarette.

Not far from where we stood was a piano. The pianist was a fat man with a mane of white hair. He turned full round as I watched and shouted to the barman. His eyes were sightless. But his playing was something to listen to.

A good number of the sports at the gaming tables were miners but there were some local citizens too and a sprinkling of trail-drivers, mule skinners and roughnecks. A tough bunch, I was thinking, when the batwing doors at the far end of the saloon swung inward and a quartet of men strolled in and stood there, surveying the crowd with all the assurance of important men. The biggest of the four drew your eye. A tall, heavy, florid-faced gent in a big hat and wearing a Marshal's star pinned to his vest. And then I saw who was with him and my heart went tumbling down into my boots. For all dressed up in two big guns and wearing a Deputy's badge on his vest was Mitch Fenton. I was that surprised I just goggled at him and it must have been then that he spotted me. A kind of hush had fallen on the folks in the bar-room when the Marshal and Fenton had come in. It deepened. You could have heard a gun drop. I saw Fenton turn his head and say something to the Marshal and that worthy gave us a long and careful scrutiny. Then without another moment wasted he snapped something at the others and they all turned round and walked out. You could have knocked me over with the usual feather, if you'd had one handy.

'Exit the Marshal and his posse,' I said to Dan. 'I figure you spotted who his deputy was.'

'Yes,' said Dan, lips drawn back from his teeth in a kind of snarl. 'I saw.'

I turned to the bulky miner next to me and tapped him on the arm.

He turned to me and gave me a hard look.

'Don't do that, stranger. It kinda makes me nervous,' he said.

'Pardon me,' I said. 'I only wanted a little information.'

'Well, what's eating you?'

'I'd just like to know the names of those two hombres who just came in and went out again.'

The miner seemed surprised that I didn't know.

'Why, that's Almighty God and the angel Gabriel,' he said, and laughed.

I laughed also, not too loud, but just politely and waited.

When he'd recovered he said, 'It was Marshal Pell and his deputy, George Berle. If you want some advice, mister, keep out of their way.'

'Yes,' I said. 'Thanks,' and I turned away.

'Have you found a place for the girl?' asked Dan.

I told him about Ma Tompkins and the house where Jeannie was now safe in bed, I hoped. I knew he'd heard what the miner had said but I figured he was being cagey and biding his time.

'Deputy George Berle,' I said softly.

'Yeah,' said Dan, 'I heard.'

I turned back to the bartender who was hovering round like a mayfly.

'Two more,' I said, and when he'd filled our shot glasses I paid him again and we drank in silence.

I don't think Dan quite knew what to do next any more than I did. Mitch Fenton with a deputy's badge on him was more than a mite different from Mitch Fenton out on the desert trail. And then the problem was taken right out of our hands by the big miner on my left. He suddenly upped his glass, drained it and then pushed his big lump of a face right up to mine and said, 'Seeing as you don't know Pell and Berle you might like to know there's a meeting about 'em at the Bonanza at midnight. Mebbe we'll see you there.' Then he turned away and followed by his friend pushed his way out of the long smoky room.

'There's trouble a-brewing in this town,' I observed.

'There's going to be a lot more trouble soon,' said Dan.

'Shall we go to the meeting?'

'I don't know, Johnny.' He pushed his hat even further back on his head. 'I'm kind of a lone wolf. Never did cotton on to working with a mob.'

'Never did have any liking for posses myself,' I said. 'Still, this bunch who're meeting at the Bonanza ain't got any friendly feelings for Mitch Fenton. I figure maybe we should go hear what they have to say.'

Dan agreed reluctantly. 'But we'll go and eat first,' he added.

So out we went at last after a few more snorts and found a restaurant called The Elite. It was run by a nice young fellow with curly blond hair and bright blue eyes. He said his name was Matt Tompkins and I asked him if he was any relation to Ma Tompkins down near the livery stable and he said he was and that she was his ma. Then he served us with hot mulligan and potatoes and dried apple pie and I began to feel a lot better. By the time we'd finished eating it was getting on for midnight. Time passes quick in saloons and eating houses, slow in prisons and parlours.

We eased out of the Elite which was across the street from the Palace. Lights still shone yellowish in the black night and a piano still tinkled in the big saloon. But the street was empty. We continued back along the street until we were about opposite the Bonanza.

'That's the place,' I said.

'O.K.,' said Dan. 'Let's go see what they have to say.'

We crossed the wide rutted street and pushed through the doors. The place was empty, save for a solitary barman polishing a glass. He gave us a long cagey look.

I went up to him. 'Where's the meeting, mister?'

'Don't know nothin' about no meeting,' he said sullenly. He sure needed a lesson in something, if only in how to speak his native language.

I leaned across the bar and put my face close to his. The trick works with some.

'We were invited,' I said.

'Don't know nothin' about no invitation,' he replied, a man of few words.

I was just beginning to feel a kind of ripple of anger go through me when a door over to his left opened and the big miner who asked us to the meeting came out.

'I heard talk.' He gave us a careful look. 'We're in the barn in the back,' he added and jerked his head in the direction of the door.

We walked round behind the bar and through a corridor. There was another door ahead of us. The miner pushed it open and we followed him into the barn. There was a group of men standing around in the hay and in the middle of them, sitting on a barrel, was a square-set man wearing town store clothes. He had a brown Derby resting on one knee. He was staring at Dan and me as we approached and something in his eye worried me. I'd seen it before in the eyes of a certain kind of lawman, not the Marshal Pell kind, but the right kind. The other men around apart from our miner friend were men of the town. I was not surprised to see the liveryman among them. Mr Sloan and Mr Michael whose shops I'd passed on the way to the Palace early in the evening would be there too, I figured. The whole place was dimly lit by two lanterns hanging from beams.

'Maybe you'd like to know something,' said the man sitting on the barrel.

The other men were all watching us closely, I noticed. They looked worried.

'As of now we know mighty little,' said Dan.

'Shoot,' was all I said.

'We know about your run-in with George Berle and his pardners,' said the man flatly. 'That's why we asked you here.' He looked at the other men. 'We figured you'd have little love for 'em.'

'You figured right,' I said. 'But how did

you know about us and them?'

'I'm William Appleton,' he replied. I looked at Dan and could see that even he was impressed. It was like someone saying, I'm the Pinkerton Agency or Wyatt Earp. William Appleton was one of the best range detectives in the West. His shadow was dark and big as a house.

'I'm being paid to track them down,' he went on. 'I followed them from Laredo to San Antone and back again into the Nueces. They're a gang and they're wanted for bank-robbing and murder all over the south-west. George Berle may have other names but it's as George Berle I want him and the men who ride the outlaw trail with him.'

'He was called Mitch Fenton in the Nueces,' said Dan grimly. 'And it's as Mitch Fenton I'll get him.'

'How come he's sitting pretty here with a deputy's badge to play with,' I asked.

'It's easy enough,' replied Appleton. 'They've got this town sewed up. The Marshal's one of their men and the citizens of Gilburg Crossing' – he threw a mean look around as he said this – 'are just about scared to death. It's an outlaw town and they know it. They're losing gold shipments just about as fast as they can dig it. Now they want

101

something done. That's why Nick Dowd is here. He represents the miners who've staked claims in the valley north of the town.'

A tall thin lantern-jawed man moved out a little into the light. 'I'm Tod Sloan,' he said. 'I own the general store here in town. Life ain't worth living any more here. We do as Marshal Pell tells us or–' he made an expressive gesture with the side of his hand against his throat. 'I for one,' he went on, 'would be mighty obligated to you gentlemen if you could help in any way to rid our community of these varmints.'

'We can't do anything,' said another man earnestly. 'We're just ordinary folks and we don't know nothing about guns. We reckoned you might be able to do something.' He stopped, then added as an afterthought, 'My name's Tompkins.' I remembered Ma Tompkins and Jeannie Bain.

It was a pattern I'd met with before. The small growing town on the edge of nowhere, the outlaws and toughs who'd taken it over under the very noses of the scared citizens. It always led to blood and grief before the mess was cleared up and sometimes it wasn't cleared up and a town just dried up and blew away in the next big wind from the north. It could happen here easy. The only hope lay in a hired detective who just had a job to do, in a man burned up with the lust to kill and a fiddle-footed outlaw with a busted right hand. The outlook for Gilburg Crossing didn't look very rosy to me. Between us we could bring it down even lower than it was.

'There's a stage out of here day after tomorrow,' said Appleton. 'It'll be carrying a gold shipment to Denver.' He made a little pit in the straw with his bootheel while we waited. 'I figured you might ride with it as shotgun guards till it's out of reach of Marshal Pell and his bunch.' Dan looked at me and I looked at him. Maybe we were both remembering this was the stage Jeannie Bain was supposed to take on her way back East.

'I'm not playing sitting-duck in a stage coach,' said Dan shortly.

'I guess we'd be happier if we watch the coach from a distance,' I said. 'We'll ride out of town before it leaves and then pick it up outside of town. We'll act escort for twenty miles or thereabouts and that ought to be enough.'

'Suit yourselves,' said Appleton. 'I'll ride around too. Maybe I can pick up something or someone.' He looked at the local men around him. 'Not a word of this to anyone, gentlemen. If we're going to bring these

103

scoundrels to justice we must proceed with very great care.'

The others began standing up and yawning and showing other signs that they were ready to go. One by one they began to trickle out until at last there was only Appleton and Dan and myself left.

'Where are you sleeping?' said Appleton.

'Out of town,' said Dan. 'I'm going back to where I left my horse.'

He looked at me, 'So long, Johnny. I'll meet you here in the morning.'

'So long, Dan,' I said and watched him cross the barn and leave by the door through which we'd come. I didn't hurry. I'd figured anyway that the barn would be as good a bedroom as anywhere else. And I had to say something to Appleton before he left.

I said it. 'I figure you might know of me, Mister Appleton. My name's Ross. Johnny Ross.' He made no answer so I went on, 'Maybe I'm not the sort of hombre who ought to sit in on this deal. There's folks who'd say I'm no law-abiding citizen.'

'Yes,' said Appleton, giving me a hard appraising sort of look out of his ice-blue eyes. 'Yes, I know a lot about you, Johnny Ross. You were a cowboy for years after the war between the states but you got kinda tired of eating plains dirt with your bacon and beans so you took to the outlaw trail. You became a gambling man and learned to play the cards so well you could beat anyone without having an ace up your sleeve. You could draw so fast you'd wait till a feller had his gun out before you'd shoot him. And never once did you shoot to kill, till that last time back in Newton when you killed Brad Owens in the Golden Nugget.'

I must have been staring open-mouthed at this story of my past for he stopped and gave me a kind of sly grin and then went on.

'Yessir. Johnny Ross. I guess there's a bit of bad in you somewhere but there's folks around the South West who'll say nothing but good of you. And if you are bad then there's no name in our language for the scoundrels we've got to deal with.' He gave me a sharp look. 'I hope we can really count on you to help.'

'Yeah,' I said, 'I suppose so. But this—' I raised my right hand— 'isn't going to be much use and the other one's still only a beginner.'

'We'll make out somehow,' he said and stood up. He yawned 'Time for sleep.' He walked over to the door leading back into the saloon and I followed him. I wanted to speak to the bartender about sleeping in the barn.

'I'll be at the Palace,' said Appleton. 'They think I'm a whisky drummer.' He went on out into the street.

'I'd kind of like to sleep in your barn, mister,' I said turning to the bartender.

He said, 'Suit yourself but mind the rats.'

'I like rats,' I said. 'They're a lot less ornery than some human beings. Let's have a last snort before I fall asleep on my feet.'

He produced a bottle and filled two glasses. I took the nearer one and said, 'Here's looking at you.' He said, 'Salud.' I raised the glass to my lips and stopped short as two flat detonations suddenly shattered the midnight quiet.

I put my glass down untouched. A cold fear gripped me. 'That was a shotgun,' I said. The barman had gone white. The glass in his hand shook and whisky spilled over onto the bar-top. I drew my Colt and walked over to the door. I peeped out. Nothing to be seen, except the empty moonlit street.

I pushed on out into the sidewalk. Not a sound, not a movement anywhere. This was a careful town in which gunshots brought no curious folk running. I turned left towards the intersection where the Palace was and then I saw something lying in the road, a dark lumpy shadow in the pale silver-lit street. I turned with foreboding clutching my heart. It was no mere shadow. It was a man. I could see a white hand stretched out in the dust. I drew nearer and before I bent down I took one long careful look around. A window went up quietly somewhere on the other side of the street. Curiosity was stronger than fear in someone.

I bent down and recognised the dark town suit, the derby hat lying a few feet away. I turned him over. The shotgun blasts hadn't left much of his face but it was Appleton and he was dead. A kind of hot anger spread through me and looking up I saw the bat-wings of the Palace saloon come open and two men stepped out onto the boardwalk.

One of them called out, harsh and commanding. 'What goes on?'

'There's a dead man here,' I said.

They came out into the pool of yellow radiance thrown by the saloon lamps. It was Marshal Pell and his deputy, whom I knew as Mitch Fenton. They approached cautiously.

'Who is it?' Pell's voice was flat. He knew the answer to the question before he spoke it.

'Maybe you know the answer better than I do,' I said.

Fenton bent down and rolled the dead man onto his back. 'It's the whisky drummer.'

107

Pell was staring at me in the dim light.

'Who're you, stranger?' he said.

I didn't like the sound of his voice. I didn't like anything or anybody at all. I had taken a vague liking to Appleton while he was picking over my past back there in the barn. And now he was lying dead in the dust with his sightless eyes staring unseeingly at the cold moon.

'You'll know,' I said, 'soon enough. Before this town's very much older I'll be looking for the hombres who gunned this man down and when I find 'em I'll kill 'em.' I gestured with the gun which I was still holding in my left hand. 'Hand him over to the undertaker and see he gets a decent burial. And if you come looking for me again, come a-smoking.'

Now there wasn't much they could do because in their hurry they'd forgotten to draw their guns so with a few muttered curses, they picked up what remained of William Appleton, ex-agency detective, and carried him away into the Palace saloon, leaving me to walk back to the barn behind the Bonanza where sleep in the straw came fitful and dream-troubled.

CHAPTER SEVEN

I usually wake fast but that morning I woke faster than usual with my hand grabbing for my gun in the straw where I'd left it before going to sleep. But it was only the saloon keeper who'd come in and waked me. He gave me a cup of strong black coffee when I went into the bar-room and when I'd rolled a cigarette, life began to run again in my veins.

A lot of problems sat on the rim of my coffee cup. The biggest of them was the girl, Jeannie. We had to get her out of Gilburg Crossing, back home to ordinary decent folk who didn't wear guns or get shot in the back. And the only way out was by stage-coach to Denver, eighty miles away in Colorado and with a gold shipment on board, like toasted cheese in a moving trap for all the local rats to smell and come a-running for. I ought to see Dan about the killing of Appleton, but Jeannie came first.

'A hell of a night,' I said, aloud, and without realising it.

'Yes,' said the saloon keeper sadly. 'It never

gets any better, does it?' He looked into a glass he was polishing as if seeking for some answer.

I thought I'd go and see Jeannie Bain as I'd promised, so I said, 'Adios' politely to my friend behind the bar and went on out into the morning sunshine.

Gilburg Crossing looked different in the morning. There were a few folks about: one or two riders passed along the street; a flat-bed wagon, driven by a tow-haired young-ster of ten or thereabouts, rumbled by. I walked on down and round the bend to Ma Tompkins' place. I climbed onto her porch and rang the bell. She came downstairs to answer it, opened the door and said, 'Who're you?'

I resisted temptation and answered politely with my hat in my hand. 'I came here last evening, ma'am, with Miz Bain. You gave her a room and I said I'd be back.'

She gave me a suspicious look and said grudgingly, 'You'd better come in.' She led the way into her best front parlour, a nice room but a mite crowded with knick-knacks and gewgaws, long lace curtains and hard plush-covered chairs.

She said, 'Sit down, young man. I'll go tell Miss Bain you're here.'

I sat down, not feeling much like a young man and more than a bit out of place. Ma Tompkins's relations stared at me out of ornamental frames. The men, I noticed, had beards and long drooping moustaches. I fiddled with my battered Stetson and felt shut-in. I was never one for sitting long in parlours.

The door opened and a face I knew looked round the door.

'Howdy,' he said, 'I'm Matt Tompkins.'

'Howdy,' I replied. 'I et in your restaurant last night.'

'Yes,' he said. 'I remember you.' He came on in and stood tall and loose-limbed in the centre of the room. 'You're a friend of the young lady who stayed here last night.'

'Yes,' I said. 'And my name's Johnny Ross. I'm thirty-one years old and I was born in Ranville, South Carolina.'

'Aw, shucks,' he said. 'You're laughin' at me, mister. I didn't mean no disrespect. It's jest – she–'

'Yes,' I said, encouragingly.

'Waal,' he said, 'I reckon she's jest about the nicest young lady I ever did see.'

He stood there looking a bit pink and shuffling his feet.

The door opened again and Jeannie Bain

111

came in. She was smiling a little in that shy way of hers and looking real good after a proper night's sleep.

'Good morning, Miss Jeannie,' I said, standing up.

'Good morning, Mr Ross. Good morning, Mr Tompkins.'

We hadn't said very much but what there was seemed pretty good to me. And then Ma Tompkins chipped in from behind her, her voice a bit harsh and nasal.

'She's off on the stage first thing tomorrow, she tells me.'

'Well, that's probably the best for all concerned,' I said. 'This is no town for a young girl like Miss Bain. I'll get your ticket from the stage-office.'

'I've told you before, Mr Ross, that I've got no folks back east,' said Jeannie. 'Why can't I stay right here? I can get work at Gilburg Crossing.'

'As a saloon girl, or worse,' I said brutally.

There were tears in her eyes then and it was a mighty big temptation to back down and tell her to stay which would be just what I would want in my goddam selfish way. So instead I hardened my heart, and it was real hard work. Even Matt Tompkins gave me a dirty look. I expect he figured I was a real mean hombre.

'I'll be here to see you onto the stage tomorrow morning,' I said. 'Meantime I should stay indoors. This town is no health resort.'

'Amen to that,' said Ma Tompkins un-expectedly. 'It's a sink of iniquity, a real Sodom and Gomorrow.'

'Gomorrah,' I said absent-minded like. My Pa never made any mistake over words from the good book. 'So-long then till tomorrow, Miss Jeannie, and look after yourself.'

And with those weak words I walked on out, avoiding Jeannie Bain's accusing eyes and wishing I had the strength to say a half of all the things I'd have liked to say to her.

I stood around in the early morning sun-light not knowing quite what to do next and then of course I remembered that I had better go find Dan Maffrey and get him wised up about last night's occurrences. I ambled on from Ma Tompkins's house to the livery stable. The owner was inside rubbing down a horse. I stood around watching him and listening to him hiss through his teeth in the peculiar way hostlers have.

'That's a fine horse you've got there, mister,' I said at last.

He broke off his hissing for a brief space

and took a quick look at me.

'Yes,' he said. 'It's a Morgan. Belongs to the Town Marshal.'

Something in his eyes as he said this, a swift flicker of double knowledge, made me think. Here was someone who'd known all about Bill Appleton and someone who'd had enough time to let Pell and his gang know about Appleton's movements and identity too. Someone maybe who'd been at the meeting. This man had been at the meeting too.

'You heard what happened to Appleton after the meeting?' I said.

'Yeah,' he said. 'I heard.'

'Someone must have arranged that,' I went on.

'Mebbe so. I jest hear things. Everyone talks to liverymen.'

'Yes,' I said. 'There's too much pow-wow-ing going on hereabouts.'

He came out from behind the Marshal's horse.

'You want your pony, mister?'

'Yes,' I said. 'I'll take a little pasear around. Maybe I'll hear a little more talk along the trail and maybe I'll find out who killed Bill Appleton.'

He went off then to get Bessie from an

inner stall. She came along and whickered when she saw me. The liveryman pulled my rig off a nail and slapped it on the mare.

'You coming back?' he said when he'd got the saddle fixed.

'I aim to,' I said, cold as a fish. 'This town kind of grows on me.'

I climbed up onto Bessie and he watched me with resentment, fear and self-disgust fighting for possession of his face. I rode out and away from town at a quiet trot. I would circle around and try to find Dan Maffrey on the other side in the hidey-hole he'd ridden off to last night.

It took me an hour to make my circle of the town. I found the trail along which Dan must have come in. It was well-worn, wheel-marked and dusty. It would be the trail up to Colorado, I figured. About four miles along, it swung north-east, twisting and turning through rough country with big rocks sticking out all round. A coach, I thought, would have to slow up some on a trail like that. I trotted on. The perfect spot lay about half a mile further on, on an upgrade that was steep enough to slow any coach to a crawl. I reined in and took a look around. There were medium-sized rocks and mes-quite bushes on both sides at the top, with enough cover for men and horses until the right moment. Further over, about four hundred yards west of the trail, the ground rose again to a ridge. I was staring at it when I heard a voice.

'You got the same idea as me.' It was Dan, of course, bellied down on the far side. I saw him stand up and then he disappeared for a moment, reappearing seconds later on his cayuse. He rode down to where I was waiting. I was thinking what a skill he had for reading my mind.

'This would be as good a place for a hold-up as any,' he said, reining in near me.

'Yes,' I said. 'It'll be here tomorrow as likely as not.' I paused. 'Miss Jeannie'll be on that coach, Dan.'

'Yes,' he said. 'I know.'

'No harm must come to her, Dan.'

'She'll be all right. It's the men who'll be after that coach I'm interested in, Johnny.'

'I know. But if lead starts flying she might be in danger.'

'That's so. But I reckon they'll be too busy shooting at us to bother with the coach and the folks in it.'

'Maybe,' I said. 'But we've got to remember that girl all the time, Dan. I feel kind of responsible for her.'

116

'Of course,' he said, giving me one of his strange looks. Then he turned the conversation. 'Let's ride over and have a look at the mining camp. After all it's them we're supposed to be working for, as well as the townsfolk and the agency detective.'

With something of a start I remembered the man who'd brought us into this business.

'Maybe you don't know about Appleton, Dan?'

'Know what?'

'That he's dead,' I said. I watched him because I was always fascinated by the way he looked when you tried to surprise him.

'Dead?' he said.

'Yes. Dead. Shuffled out of the deck. Blasted down with a shotgun outside the Palace last night.'

'Fenton or Somers,' he said.

'Or the Town Marshal,' I added.

His face was fixed, unreadable as a rock.

'Let's get over to the mining camp,' he said abruptly.

He wheeled his horse back off the trail and up the slope leading to the ridge. I followed. From the top you could see something of the wild hill country that lay all round Gilburg Crossing. The air was fresh and clear and you could see far over west and north for many miles. The real high country of the Rockies lifted up in the distance like a pale water-colour drawing. Between us and that lay a vast stretch of hills, canyons, buttes and malpais.

'The mine-workings lie north of the town,' said Dan. 'If we head west we ought to cut the trail leading from Gilburg to the north.'

So we swung west, making slow going over rough country, sliding on shale, climbing down into draws, circling a big mesa by a four or five mile valley, sandy-floored. It got hotter as the day wore on and we rested gratefully by a small creek where we watered the horses and drank enough to cure our thirst. An hour's riding brought us to a trail that we figured would lead to the miners' camp. We turned north into it, and after about four miles it led into a small canyon which opened out into a wide shallow draw. Here in a dried-up creek-bed we found the miners at work. They were scattered over a fairly wide area working singly or in pairs.

We didn't approach unchallenged. Just short of the diggings there was a roughly-built shack and as we got near someone inside bawled out,

'If you come any closer, I'll sure blow your

118

whiskers off.'

'Take it easy, mister,' I sang out. 'We don't aim to come any closer and we've got no whiskers so as you can see. Just you go and tell Nick Dowd we've come to talk to him about what happened last night.'

'Oh,' said the unseen guard. He blew a whistle then, loud and shrill. The gun barrel peeking out through a hole in the shack wall never wavered.

We sat our horses, waiting.

'Looks as though they're expecting trouble,' I said.

'Where's there's gold and women there's always trouble,' observed Dan, shifting about in his saddle. He was never long on patience.

I saw several men running down towards the shack. They were all armed with rifles. As the nearest of them came round the shack, his rifle at the ready, I saw it was Nick Dowd, still wearing his blue check shirt. He came up close, eyeing us suspiciously.

'We've come a-calling,' I said.

'Can't see no reason for calling,' he said. 'Still long as you're here you may as well stay a while. 'Light an' come on in.'

We dismounted and one of the miners who'd come along with Nick Dowd took our horses off to water. We followed Nick Dowd into the shack. They'd rigged up a stove of sorts and on it a huge blackened coffee-pot steamed. Other miners followed in at our heels. Nick Dowd found us a couple of boxes to sit on. A small man in bib overalls and a battered Derby hat fussed around the stove.

'Ain't exactly the Ritz Hotel but we've got our little comforts,' said Dowd. He introduced the men who'd come in as Roper Smith, Shorty, Mick Golightly, Swede and the Sodbuster. This last was the little hombre in bib overalls. Very soon he had tin mugs filled with hot black coffee sweetened with molasses for all and for us there were two plates of beans.

'They gives you the wind,' said the Sodbuster handing them to us, 'but it's all we got as of now, apart from a few sacks of gold dust.' He winked at his partners. They all watched us as we ate the beans. Then when we'd finished and I'd rolled a cigarette the man called Shorty said, 'You were saying when you came in that somep'n happened last night.'

'Yes,' I said. 'Something happened all right. After you'd left the meeting mister' – I looked across at Nick Dowd– 'someone cut down William Appleton outside the Palace with a shotgun.'

I paused and watched my words affect them in their different ways.

'That's sure bad news,' said Dowd, sombrely.

'It jest about leaves everything wide open for Mr Pell and his bunch,' observed Shorty. The rest of the men there said nothing but you could see they were hard hit. They were simple men who knew a lot maybe about digging for gold but were babes in arms when it came to dealing with owlhooters and desperadoes like Pell and Fenton and the rest.

'I guess we'd better hold onto the gold right hyar, Nick,' said the Sodbuster.

'Yeah,' said Dowd dubiously. 'Mebbe we'd better.'

Surprisingly Dan Maffrey came in at that point.

'If you do,' he said, 'you'll be sure asking for trouble. They'll be on your necks before you can say "knife". It wouldn't be the first time they've held up a diggings at gun point either. They've done it before and got away with it.'

'You're durned tootin', mister,' said the man called Roper Smith. 'We've got five rifles among us and a few six-shooters. But most of us ain't eddicated in shootin'. It'd be a massacre, yessir.'

'If you take a chance on getting your gold to the bank, then we'll abide by what we said at the meeting,' said Dan. 'We'll watch the stage out of reach.'

I couldn't quite see how all this fitted in with Dan Maffrey's aim to avenge himself on the Fenton bunch but still it was a handsome offer so I chimed in too.

'That goes for me, gentlemen,' I said. 'If they do try and hold up the stage, it'll be a couple or three of them, no more. I reckon we can deal with them all right.'

'All right,' said Dowd. 'We'll leave it as we planned it last night. We'll ride in with the gold at sundown, check it in at the stage office an' see it off tomorrow.'

'If you're ridin' in a couple of hours gentlemen, we may as well wait and ride with you,' said Dan courteously.

The miners seemed pretty pleased about that. Dan just sat there drinking more coffee and talking friendly-like to the men sitting around the shack. Watching him I realised again that he was a deep one, about as hard to figure as anyone I've ever ridden with.

They gave us some more coffee and we sat

around smoking and talking about mining and prospecting and other interesting subjects including President Ulysses S. Grant and then as the shadows lengthened Dowd, who had gone out with another man, came back with two heavy saddle-bags.

'That looks like a lot of gold,' observed Dan.

'Yep,' said Dowd. 'There's enough there to buy us all the whisky an' women to last us the rest of our lives.' He looked at each of us in turn. 'If you gents is ready to leave, I guess now's the time.'

We went out of the cabin and our horses were waiting. Shorty came over with an old but sturdy-looking claybank and Nick Dowd climbed up heavily into the saddle. Shorty handed up the two saddle-bags and we were ready to go. We moved off with a few shouts of 'Look after it, Nick,' and 'Keep out of the saloons,' from the little group of miners.

The ride down to Gilburg Crossing was easy even in twilight and gathering darkness. There wasn't much to talk about and maybe we were all a mite worried by the responsibility set on us. It took all of three hours to get to town, by which time it was full dusk. As we rode in the saloons were lit up and the usual sounds of festivity came out briskly into the warm night air. The stage office Nick Dowd said was over on the far side of the Palace saloon so there we rode. There was light coming from its one window. We dismounted and went with Nick Dowd onto the board-walk. He knocked on the door.

'Jud Larrabee knows we're coming,' he said.

The door opened and a man in shirt-sleeves appeared.

'You gents come with the gold?' he said.

'It's right here,' said Nick and went on into the office. I followed him and when the gold was stashed away, I bought a ticket for Jeannie to Denver.

Across the inter-section I could see the bright lights of the Palace. The white-haired ivory-banger was getting himself into trim for the evening's work by pounding out a few popular songs. It was just the time of night for a little quiet drinking.

'I figure the Bonanza'd be the safest place,' said Dan. He sure was a caution all right when it came to reading another man's thoughts.

'I guess I'll do my drinking at the Palace,' I said stubbornly 'I'm dad-burned if I'm going to be scared off by a few good-for-nothing sons like Mitch Fenton. Tonight's my night to howl and I'm going to do my howling and drinking right over there.'

'All right! All right,' said Dan giving me one of his queer cold looks. And then Nick Dowd came out of the stage office with the stage-line clerk behind him.

'The gold's all locked up in the safe till morning,' he said. 'I'm goin' to get some chuck and then I'll hit the hay. Comin'?'

I'm always ready to eat and I figured some steak and potatoes, with perhaps a nice big wedge of apple pie would make a bed for the whisky to lie on. I said, 'Yessir,' and Dan nodded agreement too. So off we trooped to the Elite Restaurant we'd eaten in the night before. The steak must have come from some old pre-civil-war mossy-horn and the apple-pie was dried apple pie with the emphasis on 'dried' but still it was chuck and we worked our way through it and drank strong black coffee on the side.

We parted in the street outside the restaurant with promises to meet at ten the next morning in time for the stage-coach departure. Nick Down went off towards the Bonanza taking his claybank with him. We mounted and rode ours down to the livery stable. The liveryman greeted us with a subdued, 'Howdy, gents.' We climbed down. I took a good look at the liveryman. He was scared right through.

'You ridin' out with the stage tomorrow?'

'As promised,' I said.

'Promises made to dead men ain't bindin',' he said.

'What's eating you, mister?' I was beginning to feel kind of irritated by the folks in Gilburg Crossing.

'Nothin',' was his reply. 'Or mebbe I don't want to be mixed up in no more trouble.' He paused and stared nervously into the dark shadows at the side of the livery barn. 'One's dead already. I don't want to be no hero.'

'You just feed and water our hosses,' said Dan, 'and leave the hero-work to us. We'll come for the hosses at half-past nine tomorrow morning.'

He nodded miserably, took the reins in one hand and led our mounts indoors. I stood there remembering Jeannie Bain. I knew we'd have to make sure she was ready to leave by the morning stage. I'd been there once before that day but I had an urge to go there again.

'Ma Tompkins's next,' I said.

Dan didn't say anything, just followed me across the road to the boarding-house. I knocked and the door opened and there was Jeannie Bain in person. She looked mighty cool and composed and seemed to be wearing a dress I hadn't seen before.

She said, 'Come in, Johnny. Come in, Mr Maffrey.'

Johnny, I thought, and Mr Maffrey. We followed her into the lamp-lit hall and so on into Ma Tompkins' parlour.

We stood there, feeling a bit uncomfortable, like a steer must feel in a race-horse stable.

'We've come to see if you're all set for tomorrow, Miss Jeannie,' I said. 'The stage goes out at ten o'clock.'

'You seem very anxious to get rid of me, gentlemen.' She sounded just a bit annoyed.

'It's not that, Miz Jeannie,' said Dan. 'We just want to make sure you're on your way back home, back east. This kind of town's no place for you.'

'Ma Tompkins says it'll be a fine town one day, with stores and churches and fine things for all,' she said softly.

'Maybe,' I said. 'But just now no better than a den of sidewinders.' I paused. 'Shucks, Miz Jeannie, we're not at all anxious to see the last of you. It's just that we're plain worried. And what's more we may even have trouble when you go. There's an even chance that the stage'll be held up on the way East.'

'If you think that, then why send me on it and expose me to danger, Mr Ross.' This was said coldly. Mr Ross, too. That cancelled out Johnny sure enough.

'There's no other way,' I said, shifting from one foot to the other. 'Also we aim to see that coach safe out of Gilburg Crossing.'

She was silent for a time and then she said, 'Very well, I'll be ready at ten o'clock.'

'We'll see you're all right, Miz Jeannie,' said Dan reassuringly. I could see he was as uneasy as I was, so I made a sashay towards the door and bumped into Ma Tompkins who was just coming in.

''Scuse me, ma'am,' I said.

'So it's you again,' she said sociably. 'Who's your tall friend?'

I introduced Dan and we exchanged a few polite remarks. Then I wound it all up by saying, 'We'll be calling in the morning for Miss Jeannie. She's leaving on the stage.'

'I've an idea the young lady don't want to leave,' said Ma Tompkins.

'We've changed her mind for her,' I said, a mite too abruptly maybe. It was time to go.

There was a chilly atmosphere in the parlour that reminded me of the high country in Arizona territory in January. I edged towards the door and Dan, for once not in full command of a situation, looked relieved.

'Good night, Miss Jeannie and ma'am,' I said and this time I got right out into the hall and so into the warmer atmosphere of the street.

'I'm not much of a hand with the fair sex,' I said.

'I'm no great shakes myself, Johnny,' said Dan.

'What we need is a couple of snorts,' I suggested and added, 'In the Palace.'

'So be it,' said Dan.

We had turned the corner now into the main street of the town and within minutes we were elbowing through the batwing doors of the Palace saloon. It was about as empty as a harlot's heart, if you know what I mean. Just a scattering of faro players, a table of poker, five men at the far end of the long bar but no miners, no cowhands, and very few of the local 'citizenry' so far as I could see. We went up to the bar and I knocked on it gently with a silver dollar. It had been a pretty busy day and it was time now to take it easy, to slow up on the spur.

A bartender ambled towards us.

'What'll it be?' he said sourly.

'Two shots of Old Crow served with a smile,' I said.

He reached down under the bar and I felt my old right hand go rigid. You never quite know what is lying out of sight below the bar counter. He came up holding a bottle of whisky and I relaxed.

'We ain't paid to smile, mister,' he said. He reached for two shot glasses and filled them.

I picked mine up. 'To a bright and happy future,' I said.

We drank and I said, 'Two more of the same, bartender. That sure hits the spot.'

He refilled our glasses and I took a look at the big mirror behind the bar. These looks prove mighty useful and once again a little caution paid off. I watched the batwings swing open and in came the Marshal, followed by George Berle as they called Mitch Fenton hereabouts, and three or four hombres I didn't know, and didn't want to either, when I considered their faces – mean enough to scare their own grandmothers.

'Trouble comin' in at the front door,' I said softly.

'Man's born to trouble,' said Dan and turned slowly round as if to meet it. This time there was no stopping and about facing. They came on in straight towards where we were standing. Maybe the demise of Mr Appleton had made them cocky. The Marshal halted about three feet away.

'Evenin',' he said civilly but in a strange grating tone.

Dan just nodded and I hurriedly pushed my second slug of whisky down the hatch. I didn't want it wasted.

'My name's Pell. I'm Marshal of this town. This is my deputy, George Berle.'

'Howdy!' I said. I gave the Deputy a hard look. 'We've met before but you had a different name then.'

The Marshal ignored this.

'You're outstayin' your welcome here,' he said. 'We'd like you to ride on – the sooner the better.'

'We're looking for three men,' said Dan. 'Name of Fenton, Somers and Willamette. They attacked and robbed me two weeks ago.'

'And where did this happen?' said Pell.

'He can tell you as well as I can. That's Mitch Fenton standing next to you,' said Dan angrily.

A small veil seemed to close down over the Marshal's eyes.

'This is George Berle, as I told you,' he said, still polite although his voice grated more than ever.

'Ask him where he was two weeks ago. Ask him about Mr Appleton. Ask him where his dry-gulching pardners are.'

Dan Maffrey was working himself up I could see. There were four hombres ranged behind Pell and his Deputy, all loaded for bear. If I let it get out of hand we'd be dead inside of two minutes and Jeannie and the miners' gold wouldn't have a cat in hell's chance of reaching Denver or anywhere else. This wasn't the time for a show-down.

I caught hold of Dan's sleeve.

'Let it be, Dan,' I said. 'It's time to mosey on.'

He shook me off and I knew we'd lose out. I pulled my gun in the nice easy way I'd been learning while Dan was getting over his wounds and I tapped him just above the temple, about hard enough to lay him out cold without really harming him. He gave a peculiar sort of grunt and sank down in a loose-limbed pile on the bar-room floor.

'Sorry, gents,' I said, 'but it's the only way. My friend suffers from pee-culiar ideas.'

They were all staring open-mouthed at our little tableau. This was my chance. I waved my gun at one of the Marshal's bunch. 'Lend me a hand,' I said. 'We'll take him outside to cool off.' The man I'd waved at came forward and helped pick up Dan. 'We'll be ridin' on tomorrow,' I said. I bent down, picked up Dan's legs and with the Marshal's man leading we carried Dan out of the Palace into the street. Between us we got him into the Bonanza and onto a table where he lay snoring slightly.

I looked at the friendly bartender. I said, 'Gimme a bottle of Old Crow.' It had been a long, busy day. I took the bottle from the bartender, sat in a chair and had a long swallow and another and another and then I fell into a deep dark hole and was asleep.

CHAPTER EIGHT

I woke up feeling as if my eyelids had turned to lead overnight. I raised my head off the table-top. Light was seeping in through the grimy glass panes of the saloon windows. I looked at the other table on which we'd laid Dan Maffrey. He wasn't there. I rubbed my eyes and peered around the bar-room but there was neither hide nor hair of Dan Maffrey. Then my ageing eyes spotted a piece of white paper on the table where he'd been. I got to my feet and made it to the table-top. Something was scrawled on the paper in lead pencil. I took it over to the window. It said,

'See you at the rondayvoo. Dan.'

I couldn't quite figure why he'd ridden off on his lonesome. He was a deep one all right, but still he couldn't spell. I heard a door open behind me. I turned slow and ready but it was only the saloon-man.

He said, 'Good morning!'

I said, 'Howdy,' and added, 'Any coffee in the pot?'

'Coming right up,' he said. 'You look as if you need it, friend.'

'I feel jist a mite lower than a snake's belly,' I said with a touch of coldness in my voice. I never have liked being told the truth. While he was out busying himself with the coffee-pot I shaped myself a cigarette. With this and a mug of coffee I felt I could face the day to come. The coffee came.

'Black as night and sweet as sin,' said the saloon-man, plonking the steaming mug down on the table.

'Yes,' I said sociably and stuck my nose in the mug. By the time I'd got through it and the cigarette I was beginning to feel like a human being again. I pulled my watch out. It said a half after eight. I needed a shave and there was plenty of time before I was due to see Miz Jeannie off on the stage. I said goodbye to the saloon-man and wandered out into the street. The sun was up. I blinked at it and turned into Bucky's Tonsorial Parlour. Bucky, a slender well-pomaded curling-moustachioed gent, was awaiting custom with a towel draped over his arm.

I climbed into his chair. He draped a white cloth round me with a flourish.

'Hair-cut and shave,' I said.

'Yessir,' said Bucky, and got to work with some dexterity. When he'd reached the stage of scraping lather off me, I tried a small question.

'You know Abe Somers?' I said.

He didn't answer straight off.

'No,' he said at last. 'Can't say I do.'

'He was having a shave here the day before yesterday in the late afternoon.'

Again the pause, careful, cagey.

'A lot of gents come in here, mister. Shaves, haircuts, beards trimmed, moustaches waxed. A few have a bath in the back room. They come dirty and they go clean. I don't ask questions.' He held my nose gently between his thumb and small finger and worked delicately around my upper lip. 'Take the Marshal, now. He's one of my regulars. Has a bath once a month. Tips like a real gent. Never asks questions, either.' He wrapped my head up in a towel, dried me off. Then came the hair-brush, pomade and a few final flourishes. 'That'll be a dollar,' he said finally with a little popping bow.

I got up, gave the tonsorial artist a dollar, put my hat on and made for the door. I turned there, knowing he hadn't finished his say.

'Abe Somers works for the Marshal. Lots of folks in this town work for the Marshal. Just watch your backtrail, mister, all of the time.'

I said, 'Thanks, Bucky,' and went on out.

I went straight to the livery stable and got my horse. She was there and in fine fettle. I felt good too, till my mind fell to brooding on the coming day. We fancy-danced our way across to Ma Tompkins'. I gave a double rat-a-tat on the front door and was greeted pretty frostily by Ma Tompkins herself.

'No need to knock the front teeth out of my door, young feller,' she said as she saw me.

'Miss Jeannie all set?' I sounded brisk, no doubt, but felt far from it.

'She's a-comin',' said Ma and sure enough there was Jeannie Bain coming downstairs with a little wicker basket in her hand and a pink hat and some kind of coat on, too.

'No need to stand there gapin' like a grey gaby,' said Ma pleasantly. 'Go and help the young lady.'

'Sure,' I said and hastened in to take Jeannie's bag.

'Good morning, Miz Jeannie,' I said. 'You're looking mighty fine.'

'Good morning, Johnny. Yes, Ma Tomp-

138

kins has been very kind to me and given me some clothes.'

'Kind – fiddlesticks!' snorted the lady of the house. 'You can't go a-travellin' lookin' like some neglected orphan.'

'You've been mighty kind, ma'am, and I wish I could thank you proper,' said Jeannie.

'Shucks,' said Ma, but I could see she was affected. Who wouldn't be by a girl like Jeannie Bain.

'We'll be on our way,' I said. We walked out onto the porch.

'Goodbye, Mrs Tompkins,' said Jeannie. Then she kissed the old girl who for once seemed at a loss for words.

We went on up the street then with me carrying the wicker basket in one hand and leading Bessie with the other. We were pretty quiet as we walked along towards the stage office. A few of the townsfolk were about now – the women carrying shopping baskets. A swamper was brushing out the Palace Saloon as we passed. We crossed the intersection and reached the stage office. Jud Larrabee, the clerk, came out, followed by Nick Dowd, carrying the gold-laden saddlebags, and said, 'Good mornin',' cheerfully.

'Stage'll be in any moment now,' he said, consulting a watch which he carried in a pocket of his vest.

I saw him look over towards the Palace and I looked too. Marshal Pell and Deputy Mitch Fenton had appeared on the board-walk outside. I looked at Larrabee. He was pale. The cheerfulness had gone. Nick Dowd looked worried. The Marshal and his deputy remained on the board-walk across the street, waiting. I suddenly felt tension building up in me, knotting the muscles of my stomach. Danger was like a strong scent in the warm morning air.

Suddenly I heard a shout. 'Stage coach comin',' and sure enough there it was round-ing the bend at the southern end of town, the dust boiling up behind it. The driver pulled the four wild-eyed, foam-flecked horses to a flourishing stop not four feet from where we stood. He stood up on his box.

'Hi-thar, Nick! Dead on time,' he yelled down. I could see the Marshal and Fenton still watching the scene from outside the Palace. Fenton turned his head, said something to the Marshal and then together they began to walk towards us.

'Got two passengers and some freight for you,' said Larrabee.

'Throw 'em in,' said the driver. Then he

spotted Jeannie in her travelling clothes. 'You wanta ride up hyar with me, lady?' He was a wild-looking hombre with huge black moustaches and a big black high-crowned Stetson to match. I could sympathise with her hesitation.

'I reckon you'd be a deal more comfortable inside, Miz Jeannie,' I said. She looked at me.

'Yes,' she said. 'I think I'll ride inside, thank you, driver.'

I opened the stage-coach door and handed her in. Nick Dowd clutching his two precious bags climbed in after her. I shut the door after them, suddenly scared of what lay ahead on the trail. Turning, I found the Marshal and Fenton standing near to Larrabee. They appeared to be watching everything attentively.

The driver cracked his whip. I looked in at the window.

'Goodbye, Miz Jeannie,' I said and was horrified to see tears rolling down her cheeks.

'Let her roll,' came the shout from above and I stood back, knowing as I had known so often before that I was too late. The coach moved off and I turned away to where Bessie was tied to a hitchrack. I slipped the reins off, climbed into the saddle.

'What's the hurry, Johnny Ross?' called out Mitch Fenton mockingly.

'See you in hell,' I shouted and spurred Bessie into a dead run out of town.

At first I followed the coach but as the last shacks slipped behind me I angled off onto the brush-covered hillside, and climbed a ridge. By steady riding I should be able to reach Dan Maffrey at our meeting place at the same time as the coach got there.

From the crest of a ridge I could see down onto the north-bound trail and sure enough there was the dust cloud raised by the passing of the coach and a good deal further along the trail than I'd expected it to be. I swung Bessie's head downgrade and put her into a canter, a long mile-eating run that had taken me out of danger more than once and now seemed likely to be taking me into it. There was a kind of benchland high above the main valley trail and I kept to the rim of this, hoping for an occasional glimpse of the coach, but, apart from one doubtful moment when I thought I saw the little swirling dust-cloud, I was unlucky. I had kept to the valley trail when I'd first ridden out of Gilburg Crossing and it had taken me a good half-hour to reach the place where

Dan Maffrey had chosen his hide-out. I judged now that I must be about level with the jumble of rocks at the head of the grade so I turned Bessie's head west, seeking a way down.

I found it, a rough twisting descent from the tableland, and as we began to climb down I heard the hard spanging echoes – two of them – rifles. I was late again and a kind of grim despair swept over me. I urged Bessie on and heard two more shots and then a third. Then there was a long fear-filled silence and suddenly I was out among rocks on the flat and there not a quarter of a mile away was the coach, at a standstill.

Dan Maffrey would be on the far side, I figured. Whoever had held up the coach would be between me and the coach. I dismounted and drew my Colt. Slowly I began to work my way forward. It was not more than a couple of hundred yards away now. I ran, crouching low, took cover behind a big hunk of rock.

Just ahead of me someone called: 'All right! Come on outa there an' keep your hands way up.'

I edged one eye around the rock and took it all in, the coach slewed across the trail, the still-steaming horses, the body of the driver slumped down in his seat and standing between me and this scene a spraddle-legged figure, back to me, in worn and dusty range-clothes, a rifle trailing down from his left hand, a Colt in his right. Ahead of the coach I saw another figure come running down from between two big rocks. No sign of Dan Maffrey. I came out into the open and the man with his back to me was only ten or twelve yards away. It was no time for weighing chances. My left hand had got to get to work.

'Don't move,' I called out clearly, 'or I'll blow a hole right through you.'

I came forward slowly, my eye on the other man still coming towards us. Maybe he hadn't figured which side I was on.

'Lie down,' I said, 'and drop your guns clear. On your face.' The man in front of me did as he was bid. I came forward and kicked his rifle and six-gun well out of reach. The other man was coming up the slight slope towards me. It was our old friend, Abe Somers. Suddenly he took in what was happening.

'What he hell!' he shouted and started bringing his gun up. I got mine in first, aiming for the centre of his body. The gun bucked and jumped like a live thing. He

144

stopped dead, screamed, spun round once and then fell flat forward.

'Hold it, Johnny,' came a yell from some way off. I knew the voice. It was old Kit Carson Maffrey in person arriving just after the showdown. He came running round the back of the stage.

I said, somewhat short, 'Where the hell've you been?'

'That can wait,' he snapped back. He stared down at the prone figure of the man who'd been over on my side of the trail.

'Who's this? Get on your feet, mister.'

The man stood up. It was Willamette.

Dan Maffrey just stood there, glaring at Willamette. But it wasn't really a glare. There was something dead about Dan's blue eyes.

He said, 'Turn around, Willamette.'

'No,' said the man and his voice was shrill with fear. 'Gimme a chanst, Mr Maffrey.' He began to babble. 'It wasn't me. It was Mitch. Him and Somers. They planned it all.' He suddenly went down on his knees. 'Look, mister, I'm a-begging for mercy on my knees.'

'That's what I was waiting for,' said Maffrey and shot him through the heart. For two or three seconds the outlaw stayed there, hunched around himself on his knees, his face a mask of horror. Then suddenly he keeled over forward and died twitching at our feet.

'We should have taken him in, Dan,' I said. 'Or you should have given him a chance to draw.'

'He didn't give me any chance,' said Maffrey and walked away towards the coach. I was aware then of another witness of the scene. Jeannie had come out of the coach and was standing near the front wheel, looking as terrified as when we'd first met. Dan seemed to ignore her. He flung open the stage door and a body sprawled out. As I ran forward I knew even without looking that it was Nick Dowd. I joined Maffrey and we stood there staring down at the dead bearded face. He'd been shot right between the eyes.

'Johnny,' said a voice behind me, 'why ever did you let me go out on the coach?' I turned to her. She was weeping quietly. Poor Jeannie, she seemed to be right out of luck all of the time.

And then came the last surprise. Dan Maffrey hadn't holstered his gun after killing Willamette and now as I looked across at him I saw the long-barrelled Colt swinging up in a slow arc and pointing straight at me. His voice when he spoke was queer, distorted.

'There's nothing in the way now, Johnny. Nothing in the way.' He was like a man talking in a dream, a nightmare.

'There's the driver,' I said, more calmly than I felt.

'He's dead,' said Maffrey. 'Quite dead.'

Even Jeannie seemed to come out of her wretchedness.

'What is it you want, Mr Maffrey?' she said, and I knew from her voice that she had sensed that there was an awful lot wrong somewhere.

And then before he could answer a shot whip-lashed the dust at our feet and a voice yelled out,

'Drop your guns and stick your hands up or by God we'll shoot to kill.'

I took one look at Dan and even then had time to be surprised at the sudden flash of fear that replaced the madness I'd read there only two minutes ago. He let his Colt fall onto the trail. I looked around and saw a rifle poking its nose round a rock. We'd been neatly out-smarted. I pulled my gun and dropped it near Maffrey's.

'What is it now?' Jeannie's voice was

quivering. I put an arm round her shoulders.

'Nothing,' I said. 'Nothing to get fussed over. Nobody'll do any harm to you, Jeannie.'

They came in then from all sides; Pell and Fenton, the four toughs who'd been behind them in the Palace on the previous night, and not much to my surprise, Noisy Nate and his pal, whom we'd last seen at the California House in Bentville. They all closed in on us with drawn guns.

Marshal Pell did most of the talking.

'We figured you were up to no good when you high-tailed it out of town,' he said, looking at me.

'Listen, Mr Marshal,' I said. 'We rode over here to protect the stage, not to rob it. We arrived just too late to stop those two men lying there from killing the driver and Nick Dowd.'

'A likely story,' he sneered. 'Now I look at it this way. You and your friend knew all about the gold shipment. He rode out and waited for the stage here and you stayed in town to make sure everything was working proper at that end.'

'That's why we killed Bill Appleton, I suppose.' My sarcasm, however, was wasted on a man like Marshal Pell.

'You killed Bill Appleton, sure; just as you killed the driver of this stage and Nick Dowd too. Then, when these two' – he swung an arm vaguely in the direction of Abe Somers and Willamette – 'arrived and challenged you, you killed them too.'

'Tried to, you mean, Marshal,' croaked a voice behind us. They all turned and there was Abe Somers, a pretty ghastly sight, his face a crimson mask of blood, getting up slowly, swaying a lot, but unmistakably alive. My bullet must have creased his front skull, knocked him out and then as he fell forward the blood must have flowed down over his face.

He shambled forward.

'That's just how it was,' he said. 'Willamette and me rid up just after they had gunned down the driver. They cut loose on us before we could even reach for our guns.'

'It's a lie. It's a lie.' Jeannie moved a step forward, speaking to Pell.

'I was in the coach. I saw it all. This was the man who held us up. He killed the driver and Mr Dowd.' She pointed accusingly at the blood-stained Somers.

And then Mitch Fenton got to work. He put out a hand and grabbed Jeannie's wrist. He pulled her towards him.

'Shut up, girl,' he said. 'You just dreamt it all.' Then he forced her down onto her knees.

I leapt forward and got in one swinging left to Mitch Fenton's jaw and then something crashed down on my head and I flickered and went out like a light into a roaring darkness.

CHAPTER NINE

I fought my way back through a swirling heaving world and opened one eye. I had a good long careful look. It was the inside of the stage-coach and opposite me sat Dan Maffrey watching me. I was not uncomfortable and wondered why. I seemed to be cushioned by something soft and warm and yielding. And then without even looking I knew what it was or rather who it was – Jeannie Bain – no less. I tried to move but couldn't. My hands appeared to be tied behind my back. The best thing to do was to wait for developments.

Jeannie must have sensed that I was back on the ball again.

'How are you now, Johnny?' she asked from somewhere just behind my head.

'Fine,' I said. 'Fine as autumn apples, as my old ma used to say. What's happened?'

'One of Pell's men pistol-whipped you, Johnny. You'd just struck the Deputy a tremendous blow when one of them came behind you. You fell all in a heap at my feet.

I thought – I thought you were dead.'

'Takes more than a pistol-barrel to kill me,' I said. 'Just wait till I get out of this coach.' I wriggled around a bit to see what I could do and discovered that my hands were tied.

'It's better not to struggle. Everything'll be all right in the end,' Jeannie said.

Dan Maffrey just sat there looking at us and my mind suddenly whipped back to that strange moment before Pell and his outlaw posse had appeared and Dan Maffrey's gun had been pointing straight at me and he'd been saying something I couldn't remember, what with this ache over my right ear. Something mighty strange it had been, some words that put Dan Maffrey on one side of the fence and me on the other. As the coach bounced and rumbled along I kept on playing with the thought, building up the whole situation like a house of cards until when I reached the last card which was Dan Maffrey's words, the whole thing flopped. It was just as the coach came to a jarring halt and I heard voices outside that I placed the last card triumphantly in place and the words came back to me and the look in his eyes too– 'There's nothing in the way now, Johnny. Nothing in the way.'

And then the door of the stage banged open and a voice said, 'Come on out,' and for the time I forgot all about the problem of Dan Maffrey.

We got out, with some difficulty, and found ourselves once more in Gilburg Crossing. We stood there surrounded by Pell's posse of gunslingers and toughs. They had climbed off their horses and now they all crowded the three of us into the Marshal's office. Pell went behind his desk, looking official, or trying to.

'You're under arrest,' he said, unnecessarily.

'Shucks,' I said, 'I figured we were going to be fêted.'

'Shut up,' said Mitch Fenton, and to underline his words he gave me a back-hander across the mouth. I heard Jeannie give a faint cry at that.

'What are we charged with?' said Dan.

'Robbing the stage-coach and murder,' said Pell.

'We're entitled to a proper trial,' said Dan. He looked pretty calm and confident but watching him I could see a small nerve jumping on the side of his forehead.

'You'll get a trial. Won't they, men?' Pell looked at his posse as he said this and they answered him with ironical grins and nods or remarks, such as, 'Sure, Marshal,' and 'You bet.'

'What's Miz Bain doing here?' I asked.

They all turned towards her, and took a look at her, and then Pell said, 'There's nothing against her. She can go her way.'

Mitch Fenton turned and whispered in Pell's ear and Pell nodded. He seemed to agree with everything that Fenton said to him.

'My deputy says he can give you work at the Palace Saloon, Miss,' said Pell.

I looked at Jeannie and was about to tell her no, not on any account, when she gave me the smallest, most imperceptible of winks and said, 'Thank you very kindly, Mr Marshal. What can a poor young woman do but accept your generous offer of help?'

The Marshal smirked complacently. 'Go help the lady over to the Palace,' he said to Noisy Nate and once again Jeannie gave me the very smallest of significant looks and went out, accompanied by the Marshal's man. The look she'd given was reassuring but I couldn't see what one young girl could do to help us in our present situation which sure was mighty ticklish.

The Marshal then grabbed a bunch of

154

keys off his desk and we were escorted into a steel-barred cell just off the main office. They thrust us in and there we were with nothing to do but wait.

We sat on our beds for a time and smoked. No one had bothered to relieve us of our belongings. No one either had said anything about chuck and as it was now well after noon I was beginning to feel plumb hungry.

'We're in a jam,' observed Dan sombrely at last.

'I've been in worse,' I said. 'And I've got out of worse.' There just wasn't any point in giving in. Also from now on I wasn't going to lay a single card down for Dan Maffrey to look at. I wasn't quite sure yet but I figured there was danger in him, danger to everyone, including himself.

I got up and took a look out into the Marshal's office. It was empty now, except for Mitch Fenton who was sitting in a chair with his feet up on the Marshal's desk top. I stood there watching him and speculating on the various methods that have been used to make a jailbreak. There was the old get-the-jailer-into-the-cell method but that was now pretty thin. Also the trick of bringing him close to the bars and grabbing him long enough to relieve him of his gun and keys.

Equally worn was the jailer-baiting dodge. This required a lot of patience and also much verbal skill and rarely paid off. Another possible method was that of setting the jail on fire but ever since Indian Pete had got himself burnt to a cinder in the hoose-gow at Santa Anna this had not found much favour among the train-robbers, murderers, road-agents and gun-slingers usually to be found locked up in various towns in the West. No, I figured something extra special would have to be thought up, special for Mitch Fenton, a hombre I liked less and less as I grew older.

'Hallo there, Mitch!' I called out.

He responded fast to his real name by looking round and shouting back at me,

'The name's Berle. George Berle. What d'you want?'

'Chuck,' I said. 'Mr Deputy George Berle.'

'It'll be coming over from the Palace – when they get around to it,' he answered.

'Thank you, Mr Berle,' I said.

He sat there glowering at me.

'How long've you been a lawman, Mr Berle?' I asked.

He just sat there pretending not to hear but I knew different. He could hear all right and inside he was simmering. Maybe baiting the jailer might succeed after all. I began to ponder out my next remark, shaping it and adding a barb here and there, when there was a knock on the door.

Mitch Fenton just sat staring for a few seconds.

'Go on,' I encouraged him. 'Go on, open up. Like as not it's the ghost of Bill Appleton.'

That one really rocked him but he got to the door and opened it. The young man from the Elite Restaurant came in with a tray of food. He stood there for a moment and Fenton said, 'Let's have a look at what you've got there.'

The young man put the tray on the desk. Fenton picked up a spoon and dug around in the two plates, obviously looking for knives, files, watch-springs or other prisoners' aids.

'Have a good look at that bread, Mr Berle,' I called out. 'There's a Gatling gun hid out in it somewheres.'

He picked up the bread, broke it in half and threw it roughly back onto the tray.

'Take it on in,' he said.

He came up to the cell-door, drawing his gun as he reached it.

'Back up,' he ordered.

I backed up. There isn't much else you can

do when you're looking down the muzzle of a Colt .45.

Fenton then produced a key and unlocked the door. He motioned the young man inside. And then with him standing between me and Fenton I saw his eyelid droop and the little finger of his left hand wriggled an unmistakable signal. I put out my hands to take the tray and felt the small folded square of paper held against the wood. The young man let go and turned away.

'Get goin',' said Fenton irritably. It was almost as if he sensed something not quite according to Hoyle on jail etiquette. The young man moved out and Fenton slammed the iron grille with a clang. Then he turned the key, withdrew it and marched back to his desk. He dropped the key on the top.

Busying myself with the tray I slipped the note into a vest pocket. Then we got down to the important business of eating. They'd provided some kind of stew, not bad, bread and there were two good-sized wedges of dried apple-pie. Although I was pretty anxious to read what was in the note I ate slowly. Dan Maffrey had remained pretty silent ever since we'd been thrown into the hoose-gow and even now he was far from sociable. I didn't mention the note. I wasn't sure just how far I could trust him now.

My moment came when I'd finished eating and it was time to have a smoke. I drew out my sack of Bull Durham and instead of a cigarette paper I flattened out the note in the palm of my hand. It wasn't much bigger than a cigarette paper. On it the following message was written in small neat handwriting:

'BE REDDY AT SEVEN. J.'

Ready, or reddy, as Miz Jeannie had spelt it, for what? It could of course mean only one thing. Somehow or other she was going to help us out of jail. I took a look at my watch. It was ten after three. Nearly four hours to kill. Or maybe be killed. I decided to let Dan in on the secret, strange as he had now become.

I took a look through the grille which separated us from the main office. Mitch Fenton was cleaning a six-gun. Another one lay within easy reach on the desk top. He was whistling unmelodiously.

I put a finger up to my lips and held out the scrap of paper towards Dan. He took it and read it carefully. Then he looked up and nodded. I held out my hand and he passed

159

back the note. It was a dangerous thing to leave lying about – dangerous for Miz Jeannie, I figured. So I wadded it up and chewed it for a while till it was just pulp again, then I rubbed it well into the earth floor of our cell and no one could have told what it was or ever had been.

Time, as I have already observed, passes mighty slow in prison and the next three hours were pure ornery hell. Dan Maffrey seemed to take it for granted that I would stay awake and fell into a sound sleep, snoring a bit, a weakness that I find makes me laugh. I wanted to sleep myself and even dozed off once to wake with a start a few minutes later. I got up after that and walked around a bit. Then I smoked a cigarette, noting as I rolled it that I had enough tobacco for only two more. Light began to fade and Mitch Fenton finished cleaning the gun. He got up and lit an oil-lamp on the desk. Now and then he threw a mean glance in my direction.

Then came the first interruption. There was a sharp rat-tat-tat on the door. Mitch Fenton went to open it with a gun in his hand. The visitor was Abe Somers. He come on into the office. The top of his head was bandaged.

'The Marshal figured it was time to relieve you for a spell, Mitch,' he said.

Fenton just grunted and reholstered his gun. I looked at my watch. It was a quarter after six.

'Keep a careful eye on 'em, Abe,' Fenton said as he moved towards the door. 'That little one's an Injun.'

I made the Apache sign with my thumb and finger as he looked across in my direction and he snarled back at me like a treed mountain lion. Then he went on out and Abe Somers swaggered across to within about three feet of the grille, forgetting to lock the door after Fenton.

'Howdy, Abe,' I said affably. 'Still doing the dirty work for the Marshal?'

'You sonofabitch,' he said. 'You won't be so cock-a-hoop when you're a-dangling from the end of a rope.'

'Very true,' I said sadly. 'Howsomever, Abe, we've all got to die some time. How's your head?'

Like Mitch Fenton, Abe wasn't strong on repartee. He just growled and turned away. I looked back at Dan Maffrey but he was still hunched up on his bunk wandering about somewhere in his own mighty peculiar world. Some folks go kind of scatty if you

161

shut them up behind bars and I figured Dan Maffrey was one of them. I turned my attention back to Abe Somers and saw with some pleasure that he had produced a bottle of red-eye and even now was filling himself a mugful.

'Salud, Abe,' I called out. 'May all your troubles be big ones.' He stood there watching me balefully for a long moment, then he drank, smacking his lips and generally trying to show me how good it was. Abe was the kind of man who'd enjoy pulling the wings off butterflies.

He put his empty mug down and rolled himself a smoke. When he had it going nicely he refilled his tin mug again. He drank, more slowly this time but still steadily. Things were panning out well. A couple more slugs of red-eye and ole Massa Somers was going to be ripe for plucking. As time oozed by I began to feel the tension mounting almost unbearably in me. I turned my back to Abe and had a peek at my watch. Two minutes to go.

Suddenly I heard a high shout somewhere out back of the jail. Abe Somers put his mug down and began slopping more whisky into it. The door was behind him. Very slowly it began to open. Abe Somers raised the mug to his lips. There was another yell from somewhere outside. This time it was clear to hear. 'Fire!' Somers stopped raising the mug and listened. A slim figure slipped through the half-open door behind him. I picked up a tin plate off the tray and banged it against the bars. Somers stared at me with the slightly glass-eyed look of the half-drunk. The newcomer had a gun in his right hand. His right hand! HER right hand! It was a girl. It was Jeannie Bain. She raised the gun high, stepped up behind Abe Somers and brought it down with a smart crack on the top of his head. He just sighed and slumped onto the office floor.

'The key's on the desk-top,' I yelled.

She grabbed it, ran forward and slipped it into the lock. She turned it and the door swung open.

'Quick,' she panted. 'The Palace is on fire. There's two ponies behind the jail.'

'Come on, Dan,' I said. 'Thanks, Jeannie.' I stared. This was a very different Jeannie from the one I'd known before. Her hair was tousled and of all things she was wearing pants – a thing I don't hold with in pretty young women.

I said, 'Where did you get those pants from?'

163

She laughed. 'You've got about two minutes' start of Kingdom Come and you waste time worriting over pants. I got 'em from Matt Tompkins. Now get going or you'll never live to tell the tale.'

'Yes'm,' I said meekly and looking around saw our cartridge belts and guns hanging from a nail on the wall. I grabbed them off and handed Dan his. I strapped mine on and immediately felt better. A man gets to feel kind of naked without his shooting iron.

'Right,' said Dan. 'Let's get out of here.'

We slipped out through the door and sure enough over on the other side one end of the Palace was blazing merrily. Men were hurrying about with buckets and some horses stampeded along the main street.

'Round back,' I said, and we cut in behind the jail and there sure enough were our two horses all ready saddled, sniffing the smoke-filled air uneasily and raring to go.

Jeannie stood back against the wall of the jail as we climbed into our saddles. I gave her a wave and headed out into the street. We came out into a full glare of light and a voice from the broad walk suddenly yelled.

'They've busted out of jail.'

I drew and put a shot somewhere above the man's head. Men shouted and I could

164

hear a horse coming at a gallop. Then someone started firing. I swung Bessie's head
and, followed by Dan Maffrey, went out of
town at a dead run. Bessie needed no spur.
The fire, smoke and general hubbub was
enough and Dan Maffrey was hard put to it
to keep up with us.

'Circle around,' I yelled at him. 'It's a
cinch they'll figure we're heading due north
for the miner's camp. We'll outsmart them
and come in from the north.'

'Right,' he said, and we settled down to
the job of keeping a good distance between
ourselves and any possible pursuers.

'If we keep moving at this pace we can
stick to the trail most of the way and then
circle round the camp,' I said.

Dan's only answer was to urge on his
horse and we were soon well along the
northern trail out of town. After another
fifteen minutes' riding I figured it was time
to listen in on any pursuit.

'Hold it,' I shouted to Dan and reined in.
When the air was still I cocked an ear south-
wards. For a moment I wasn't sure and
then, finally, I could hear it. The insistent
beat of hoofs – not one horse, I reckoned,
but probably four or five.

'They're on their way,' I said.

'Yes,' said Dan, 'I can hear 'em. Quite a little bunch of 'em by the sound.'

'A few more miles,' I said, 'and we'll branch off East of the camp and come in as I said from the other direction.'

'Let's go,' he said, and we spurred off up the trail. The horses were well rested and still fresh so we covered a lot of ground. When we left the main trail of course things would be different and we'd be slowed up some. When the few miles were covered I shouted to Dan, 'This is where we head east,' and I turned Bessie's head away and immediately began to climb. We were on the lower slopes of a long meadow leading gradually up to a ridge crowned with live oak. One could just see enough as the full moon was well up in the sky. We halted on the ridge and listened again. Once more the distant drumming of hoofs was audible. We rode on following the ridge top with the trees as a screen. You can be seen against a sky-line almost as well on a moonlight night as by day. The line of the ridge was roughly north-east and I reckoned that in another half-hour or so we ought to be abreast of the mining camp. Something was nagging away at me now and for a time I couldn't place what was worrying me. And then suddenly I

166

knew. We'd been so preoccupied with getting away from town that I hadn't had time to think about it. Jeannie was the worry.

'I'm sure worried about Miz Jeannie,' I said aloud. 'If anyone saw her dodging around the Marshal's office she'd be suspect right off.'

'Yeah, she would,' was all Dan Maffrey said. Now this irritated me. He just didn't show enough concern for someone who, after all, had saved our lives.

'If they've got Jeannie Bain,' I said, 'it alters everything.'

'Nothing's altered,' he said, reining in, and the moonlight fell full on his large smooth dangerous face. 'For me, there's just Mitch Fenton and Abe Somers.'

'Only the girl matters and her safety,' I said softly. 'She comes first.'

'All right, all right,' said Dan. 'But don't ever get in my way.' I gave Bessie the rein and moved on slowly. I knew at that point that Dan Maffrey and the bug in his brain didn't mean anything to me any more. He and I were quickly approaching the end of the trail. And it looked like that trail would end in grief for some. We rode on then, the land taking us away from the main trail to the camp and then after another half-hour I

167

saw it shining faintly in the long valley where they'd found the gold. We were now well to the north and we circled in on the camp, knowing that the pursuit would go no further, if so far. We approached cautiously but were challenged just short of the main valley by a miner with a gun. He called out from behind a rock, 'Who's there?'

I said, 'It's Johnny Ross and Dan Maffrey.'

'O.K.,' he called. 'Come on in but keep your hands off of yore guns.'

We turned the rocky outcrop and there he was with the Winchester cradled in his arm.

'I'll follow you down to the hut,' he said. 'There was folks enquiring after you only fifteen minutes back. We sent 'em packing – Marshal Pell and his goddam gunmen.'

We rode quietly down to the hotel where we'd first talked to Nick Dowd and the others. We dismounted outside and went on in. The miners we'd met before, Roper Smith, the Sodbuster and Swede, were there. They were all armed and in an ugly mood.

'You've heard what happened to Nick Dowd?' I said.

'We've heard,' said Roper Smith. He stared hard at me in the dim lamplight. 'We've also heard that you two men killed him.'

'From Marshal Pell?' I said.

168

'Yeah, from Marshal Pell.'

'Maybe you'd like our side of the story?' I said.

'I reckon it's owing to us,' said the Sod-buster grimly.

I said, 'O.K.' and I told them the story right from the beginning when we'd first met up in the New Mexico desert country. It took some time a-telling and when it was over there was a long silence. Then Roper Smith stood up and came forward. He held out a hand to me and I shook it.

'You sound honest,' he said. 'Pell sounds like a liar.' It was as easy and straight as that. 'The gold's somewhere in the Palace or the Marshal's office. We aim to go down there tomorrow at dawn an' collect it. We'd be sure obliged if you two gents would come with us and help get back what belongs to us.' He paused. 'It ain't goin' to be easy and like as not will end in gunplay. What say? We want the man who killed Nick Dowd.'

'We're with you, sure,' said Dan, speaking for the first time. 'But one thing I ask. No one comes between me and Mitch Fenton or Abe Somers. They're my business.'

They mumbled their agreement to this and didn't see what I saw in the eyes of Dan Maffrey.

I said, 'There's a girl mixed up in all this.'
'Whenever there's trouble you'll find a woman somewhere in it,' said the Sodbuster.

'She's done no harm to anyone,' I said. 'As I told you she got us out of the calaboose. All I want to say is if there's any gunplay, make sure the girl's nowhere around.'

'It ain't likely,' said Swede, 'seeing as we've decided to jump 'em at first light.'

This seemed good sense so I said no more but I was worried and I went on being worried after we'd bedded down for a few hours' sleep. There was something wrong with the shape of things. The pattern wasn't as it ought to be.

CHAPTER TEN

Someone shook me awake and it was still full dark. I got up, yawned and stretched and suddenly remembered yesterday's happenings and what lay before us. The idea aroused no pleasure. Maybe I was beginning to feel old or maybe I just wanted to have done with excitement and settle down nice and quiet-like. I went outside and found someone with a fire and a big black coffee-pot. I looked at my watch. It was only four o'clock, which was the hour we'd fixed. Even the stars looked sleepy. The Sodbuster who was tending the fire gave me a mug of coffee and I helped myself to molasses from a jar he had there. Other vague figures, among them Dan Maffrey, came into the fire-light. No one said much. It was too early in the morning. Then Roper Smith came up. He had some coffee and then he said,

'The hosses are all waiting. I guess we'd better get movin'. The earlier we're there, the more chance we have of catchin' 'em with their pants down.'

He paused and then continued, 'There's twelve of us and maybe more of them. But we've got the advantage. I figure we ride in, grab the Marshal – he sleeps in the Palace – and force him to hand over our gold. After that all we've got to do is ride out.'

There was a murmur of agreement from the dark figures around the fire. I suddenly thought they'd forgotten something.

'What about the man who murdered Nick Dowd?' I said. It seemed kind of important to me that something should be done about that.

'Yes,' said the miner called Shorty. 'There's that.'

There was a silence and I knew they didn't really want to do anything. They were all scared of guns and they knew that such a thing as law and order just didn't exist in Gilburg Crossing. They also knew they didn't stand a chance against men like Pell and Fenton and Somers who had forgotten more about guns than these miners had ever known.

Dan Maffrey said, 'Leave the killers of Dowd to me.' Just that. No more. His words seemed to hang over us like a cloud. Something in the way he said them, I guess.

'Time to ride,' I said, breaking the silence. Slowly the group dispersed from around the fire and went around the shack to where the horses were waiting. Following them I felt worried. Somehow I couldn't see them in a gun-battle with the Marshal and his gang of toughs. I found Bessie who snorted with pleasure as I came up. When I mounted she crow-hopped around and tried her usual tricks to show that this was her idea of fun. Then she settled down and we joined the band of miners heading down the trail for Gilburg Crossing.

I found myself riding side-by-side with Dan Maffrey, looming large in his saddle and as silent as ever. We rode on for a time in the pre-dawn blackness and then slowly light seemed to grow up out of the ground on all sides. I could see the faint outline of the canyon rim and then as we debouched onto the benchland the eastern sky paled and one by one the stars turned out their lamps. It's always a good moment, the beginning of another day, full of some kind of hope and promise. Very soon the pale eastern sky warmed up with the red light of dawn. A bird woke up and started its morning exercises and men in the little cavalcade began to talk a bit. It was going to be tricky,

I thought. We'd got to get there in time to surprise Pell and his men. We rode on, still at what seemed to me to be a mighty slow pace. Then suddenly ahead of me, I could see the outlines of the town, the first shacks and, standing up above them, the solid bulk of the two-storeyed Palace Saloon. Everything was still, pale-coloured and quiet.

We reached the first house and Roper Smith held up a warning hand. We all reined in and he whispered back to us, 'We'll leave our mounts here and come in on the Palace from both sides. Let's go.' We tethered our ponies near a shack with a hole in the roof. Then we all trooped quietly down the slight grade heading to the saloon. Sunlight suddenly gilded the roof-tops in front of us. Approaching I looked at the Palace and saw the effects of the fire Jeannie Bain had started. It had burnt out one room on the first floor but otherwise had done little damage. There was no sign of life anywhere.

'We divide here.' Roper looked at Maffrey, 'You go round the back with five others. The rest of us'll use the front door.'

Maffrey led off five of the miners and I went with Roper Smith and six others to the front. A cock crowed as we cat-footed our way to the entrance and I jumped a little, my left hand clutching my gun. I drew it. Roper Smith pushed open the bat-wing doors leading into the saloon. We followed close on his heels. The big room was empty and the rank smell of burning was strong.

'They'll be sleeping upstairs, if they're here,' said Roper Smith.

We found the staircase behind the bar. They must hear us, I thought. Eight men make a lot of noise even when they're trying to be quiet. We got to a landing with some doors leading off it. Roper Smith had a shotgun in his hands and he walked up to the door and kicked it open. We followed in. A man in long-horn underwear sat up in bed, his eyes bewildered.

'What the hell?' he croaked.

'Where's Pell and Fenton?' said Roper Smith.

'They ain't here,' said the man on the bed. He tried to look tough but it isn't easy when all you've got on is underwear.

'Just tell us where they are or we'll blow your head off,' said the Sodbuster.

'I don't know nuthin',' said the man. 'I'm just a bartender.'

'He's lying,' said Maffrey, and leaned forward and raked his gun-sight down the man's cheek. He gave a light whining sort of cry and fell back across the bed.

'If you want any more of the same, by God, you can have it,' said Maffrey.

'No, no,' the man cried out. 'They're down at the Marshal's office. They're there. In the jail, the hoose-gow.' Words came tumbling out in his eagerness to be rid of us.

'Right!' said Roper Smith. 'We'll go on down there an' dig it out of them.'

We trooped out again and I thought by this time most of the town must know about the invasion, seeing as we'd left the horses right outside the Palace. The street, however, was still quiet and deserted. We crossed the intersection towards the Marshal's office and everything looked like an easy victory. Then Wham! Bang! came two shots. One hit Shorty and tumbled him flat in the street, the other skitted past my feet sending up little snakeheads of dust.

Maffrey yelled out, 'Scatter,' and we all did, except that Roper Smith bent over Shorty, heaved him up under one arm and took him into cover along with the others. Cover was the Stage office for some; the Palace for others. Those who'd hid behind the Stage office made a run for it after five minutes and joined us in the Saloon. And there we were, some thirteen men all nice and snug like rats in a trap. There had been fourteen but Shorty was dead.

'What are we a-goin' to do?' asked the Sodbuster. And it was as plain as the big nose on his own homely face that neither he nor any of the other miners knew how to set about smoking out Pell and his curly wolves.

I said bluntly, 'There's one of two ways. We either burn 'em out or rush 'em under covering fire.' I looked round the circle of tired, bewildered faces. 'Who'll volunteer to help me rush the front door?'

For a moment no one said anything. Then Dan Maffrey said, 'Okay. I'll side you, Johnny.'

'Right,' I said. 'Now listen and listen good. I want three or four of you to stay here and space yourselves out. Three or four can run over to the Hardware Store on the other corner. You can get there by going back down the street and cross over when you're out of range. The same goes for the other three who can cover us from the Stage office. We'll give you fifteen minutes to get there. Set your watches by mine. It's now twenty after seven. At exactly twenty-five minutes before eight you open up with all you've got and ventilate the hoose-gow from hell to breakfast. And for the love of Mike remember that when we start running over there, Dan and me, that we're your friends. There's no call to ventilate us.'

They grinned a bit at that and started to divide up. The Sodbuster took three of his pals out through the far end of the Saloon. The miner called Swede went with two more, as I had said, down the street towards the Livery Stable. I watched them cross and disappear. They'd find their way up to the Hardware Store. The rest began to space themselves out in the Palace, taking up positions at windows on the floor above. Dan and I were left standing near the entrance.

'As soon as the guns begin to pop,' I said, 'we run straight across to the corner and get flat against the wall. The firing will keep their heads down so we should be all right.'

'How much time's left?' said Dan. There were drops of sweat on his forehead. I took a look at my watch. 'Just eight minutes.' There was time for a smoke, I figured, so I built myself one and had a few thoughtful drags. One gets mixed up in all kinds of adventures but never before had I been caught up in something that meant so little to me as this one. And then I remembered Bill Appleton and his few kind words and how he'd died and how all those miners had scrabbled away for gold for a mighty long time, only to have it stolen by a lot of good-for-nothing sons like Pell and Fenton. I took a last long drag at my cigarette, then dropped it on the floor and ground it out with my boot-heel. I looked at my watch. A half-minute to go. No, I thought, you owe a debt to someone and this is how you pay it. I turned to Dan.

'You all set?' I said.

'Yeah!' he said and grinned, but it was a death's head grin at that. 'All set.'

The minutes suddenly began to sound off in my head like the strokes of a big bell. The death bell, I thought, and then suddenly there was a burst of gunfire from some-where across the street and another.

'Let's go,' I said, and we ran full tilt through the bat-wing doors and diagonally across the street to the corner wall of the Marshal's office. At a time like that you remember details. The next thing I knew I was flat up against the wall of the jail and the gunfire had stopped. Now we wanted a lot more covering fire to help us through that front door and even then it looked like suicide to attempt to get in that way. Pell and the others would just blow holes through us once we stepped through it.

And then quite suddenly someone – Pell, I think – shouted out through the window.

'You can give up any fool notions about rushing the jail. We've got the girl in here with us. We'll kill her if you put a foot on the doorstep.'

I felt myself go pale while he was speaking. There was no mistaking the menace in Pell's words. He and the others were desperate men and I knew there wasn't a cat in hell's chance for Jeannie Bain if we tried anything. We were really out on a limb now. I leaned my head against the wall and suddenly all the excitement drained out of me and I felt sick and tired. I turned my head and looked at Dan Maffrey. He was white and his eyes had got that mad empty look I'd seen in them before.

'What now?' My voice was dry as a corn-husk.

'Kick the door down and go in shooting,' he whispered back.

'No,' I said flatly. 'Not with the girl in there.'

There was a flame, a wicked one, in his eyes but no wickeder than the flame in me. We stayed there a long minute staring at each other and then suddenly he backed down.

'Have it your own way,' he murmured.

'Make up your minds fast,' said a voice from inside. Fenton's, I thought.

'If you ain't done thinking in two minutes from now. We'll take it out of the girl.'

I looked across the street to where all the others were hiding and beyond I could see that the town was now broad awake and watching. I could see folks in windows and on roof-tops. This was the biggest show they'd ever seen. I made up my mind.

'The girl's in there with 'em,' I yelled across in the direction of the Palace. 'We'll have to let 'em go.'

'Not with our gold,' a voice yelled.

There was a pause. Then the Marshal shouted out of the nearest window.

'All right. Promise us a safe conduct out of town and we'll leave the gold here on the doorstep.'

'That's a bargain,' came a shout from the Palace.

'We'll take the girl as a hostage as far as the end of town. We give you our word we'll leave her safe and sound there.' It was Pell speaking again.

I was about to protest when back came the answer from the miners.

'We'll take your word for it.'

181

There was not much I could do then but I gritted my teeth and swore privately I'd kill every one of 'em if they hurt a hair on the girl's head.

'We're moving away from here,' I called out and did so at once, Dan following me out into the middle of the road. They could have shot us down then but no one tried. Instead Pell came out onto the broadwalk.

'I'm sending a man for our horses,' he said.

'Send him,' I said.

It was our old pal Noisy Nate who emerged then, looking pretty scairt but trying hard to hide the fact. He went off in the back of the jail and appeared five minutes later with another man and seven led horses. We had moved back to the broadwalk outside the Palace by this time and the miners had come out and joined us. We just stood there watching while they all came out in a bunch, six of them and Jeannie. Everything was dead quiet now. Pell suddenly came forward with two saddlebags of gold. He put them down on the edge of the broadwalk. Then slowly he walked to his horse and swung up into the saddle. The rest of the gang mounted. I watched Mitch Fenton help Jeannie up behind him. Then still slowly, they all wheeled into position and began to move across the road towards us and the main street leading west past the saloon, the barber shop and the livery stable round the bend.

Suddenly the Sodbuster ran forward towards the two saddle-bags. He was going to make sure. I switched my attention to the gang. They were moving into a trot. They were already abreast of the Tonsorial Parlour. A yell from the Sodbuster split the quiet.

'They've got the gold. This is just rocks.'

Everything just went all to hell in a second. The gang spurred their horses into a dead run. Guns seemed to explode on all sides. I ran out, triggering off a shot as I did so.

For a moment I thought, by God, they've got away with it, and felt the full sense of defeat and despair. Then suddenly even as I ran I saw them all come to a sliding halt and beyond them I could see why. A great big hay-wagon had pulled right across the street and shut off their escape route. Someone let off a couple of shots from the top of the wagon. A horse reared up high and its rider came tumbling off. Then they all turned and drove forward in a bunch, shooting. Miners and townsfolk fired back. Two outlaw horses went down and my heart seemed to turn over as I thought of Jeannie Bain. I ran out, Dan Maffrey with me. I saw Mitch Fenton and a few yards away Jeannie's blue dress. I got nearer – my gun out.

'All right,' I yelled. 'Give up.'

'No, by God,' I heard Dan Maffrey shout. 'They're mine.' He fired once from over to my right and there was an answering shot from Fenton. Turning I saw Maffrey's gun fall out of his hand. He went after it onto his knees in the dusty street.

'No,' he yelled again. 'No, I give in.'

He was staring wildly at Mitch Fenton. 'Mercy,' he yelled. 'Mercy.'

I was aware even then of a big fair-haired figure picking Jeannie up out of the dust and I knew she was safe.

'I'm a-waiting, Fenton,' I said, and drew his attention away from Maffrey. I watched his gun come up and I fired just as it rose. The bullet seemed to hit him square in the chest, the impact raising him up on his toes. For a split second he teetered, then his gun roared and the bullet hit the ground at his feet. He slumped down then and lay quite still. I was still aware of confusion around me and whirled to meet whatever might be coming, but the fight was over. A little way off three of Pell's gunmen were standing with their hands up and looking plumb scared. Miners stood around in a wide circle. Further away Abe Somers lay twisted and broken.

I saw the Sodbuster and said, 'Where's Pell?'

He wiped a hand across his dirty face.

'He ain't here, by God,' he said, staring around.

'Then he's got away with your gold, after all,' I said.

'No,' he said. 'No.'

He turned round, shouting at the other miners.

'Pell's got away. After him.'

Three horses were still standing just outside the centre of trouble, Roper Smith, the Sodbuster and another miner ran towards them.

'Which way?' shouted Roper Smith.

Matt Tompkins showed up then.

'He rode round the hay-wagon just as I was carrying Miz Bain out of harm's way,' he said. 'I figure he's heading west or south.'

'Get some more horses an' come after him,' shouted Roper Smith.

Several men ran off towards the Livery

Stable. I left them to it. They'd either catch Pell or they wouldn't. I didn't much care either way. I had other things on my mind. I looked round to see what had happened to Dan Maffrey. He'd disappeared and I thought maybe that was the best for all concerned. Most of them had seen him get down on his knees to Mitch Fenton and some had heard him beg for mercy. Maybe he was plumb ashamed of himself and deep down inside I was ashamed too, as if some of his fear had rubbed itself off on me.

I walked towards the hay-wagon then, looking for Jeannie Bain. She was there all right, with Young Matt Tompkins hovering around her like an anxious bumble-bee.

I said, 'You all right, Jeannie?'

'I'm all right, Johnny,' she said. 'And thank you more than I can ever say for helping me.'

'Shucks,' I said. 'If it hadn't been for Matt here you might have been way up in the Sangre di Christo high country by now.'

'Yes,' she said looking up at him. 'Yes, he sure saved my life. How can I repay you, Matt?'

'Well,' he said simply, 'you could marry me, Miz Jeannie, and then I figure we'd be quits.' He gave her a long and very loving look which she returned, I noticed, in full measure. I knew then that any vague hopes I'd ever had of marrying Jeannie Bain were doomed. Young Matt Tompkins was the man in her young life all right and he sure was a fast worker.

'What brought you and that hay-wagon out into the street just at the fitting moment, Matt?' I said.

'Well,' he drawled, 'I sure couldn't accept the idea of Jeannie here bein' taken off as a hostage. There's no trustin' folks like Pell and the others. I remembered that Granpaw Tranter had brought a hay-wagon into town last night. I figured if I could get it out across the street in time I could hold 'em up an' maybe shoot some of 'em before Jeannie came to any harm. Mebbe it was a fool notion but it worked.'

He just stood there tall and gangling and honest and I liked him. He and Jeannie would be all right.

'Right,' I said. 'You take Jeannie back to your Ma's house. I'll be seeing you.'

'Sure,' he said. 'Come on, Jeannie.'

They walked off then down the street towards Ma Tompkins' boarding house and I turned round and took a look at what was going on. The excitement was over and the crowd that had gathered was losing interest in the dead bodies of Mitch Fenton, Abe Somers and a third man whose name I didn't know. A small band of people were hustling what remained of Pell's gang in the direction of the jail. An old man who I guessed must be Grandpa Tranter, started backing the hay-wagon into the alley out of which Matt had driven it only a short while ago.

There wasn't much to do so I wandered into the Bonanza Saloon and said 'Howdy' to the bartender. Considering all that had been going on just outside his front door, as it were, he looked pretty calm.

'A posse's gone out after Marshal Pell,' I said.

'That feller kin ride,' he said. 'An' he knows the country. They'll be lucky if they get him.'

'Yes,' I said. I began to build myself a cigarette. But my fingers were jumpy and after a while I gave it up and threw away the bits.

'You look as if you could do with a drink, Mister,' said the bartender.

'Yes,' I said, 'I reckon I could. Have one yourself.' He reached down below the bar-top and fetched up a bottle of Old Crow and a couple of glasses. He filled them carefully. Then he pushed mine across and raised his own.

'I can't think of anything to drink to,' he said.

'The future of Gilburg Crossing,' I suggested, and then as has happened so often on my twisted trail there was a sudden yelling and shouting out in the street. A real old hullabaloo. Just something to get between me and a nice quiet drink.

I raised my glass again. 'To the future of Gilburg Crossing,' I repeated and drank it down. Then I turned away and went to the door to see what the present of Gilburg Crossing had to offer. As I had half-suspected it was the posse back in triumph with the former marshal of the town riding in their midst, his hands tied to his saddle-horn. The citizenry were out in force now, shouting praises of the posse or abuse of the Marshal. Neither mattered much, I thought, looking at them. If the Marshal suddenly got free with two guns and his bunch they'd run like rabbits. I decided to see what would happen and followed the procession over to the jail.

CHAPTER ELEVEN

They had Marshal Pell tied to a chair when I got into the jail and were shouting accusations at him from all sides and getting nowhere. There were men there I'd never seen before, all pretty brave and confident, now that the Pell gang, as they called them, were either dead or under lock and key. Roper Smith was in there along with the Sodbuster, Swede and other miners. He didn't look too pleased with the way things were going and suddenly I saw him get up on a chair and start shouting for attention. He got it at last by firing his six-gun through the roof. That calmed the mob. He spoke briefly and they listened.

'We ain't gettin' anywhere, folks, by yelling at the prisoner. There's only one way to deal with him and that's to try him an' then hang him.'

They gave a yell at that and someone in the crowd shouted: 'O.K., Roper, you're the judge.'

Standing just near Roper was the storekeeper, Tod Sloan. He held up a hand and the crowd quieted again.

'This isn't legal,' he said flatly. 'You can't just make anyone a judge and try a man for his life. It ain't constitutional.'

I reckoned he had a point there. A judge is a judge, not a miner. One of the miners came forward.

'We oughter take him to Durango an' see he's tried proper,' he said.

This made the crowd yell with anger.

'We'll try him now and hang him and take him to Durango after,' shouted the Sodbuster.

This went down well and vague protests from Tod Sloan and his one supporter were disregarded. Roper was put in a chair at the ex-marshal's desk. The Sodbuster was made prosecuting attorney and the miner who'd wanted Pell to have a proper trial was defence counsel. His name was Morland. They all wrangled a bit over the jury and when they were chosen there weren't many more left to sit in the court. However, word about what was going on had spread and before long the room was crowded with the citizens of Gilburg Crossing.

Roper opened the proceedings with a few words about Pell, explaining what he'd done, bringing in the deaths of Appleton and Shorty and Nick Dowd and dwelling on the theft of the gold. He also mentioned Mitch Fenton and the others and how they'd come into town not more than a couple of weeks back and helped Pell to over-awe the town. They'd found the saddlebags on Pell's horse when they caught up with him.

Then the Sodbuster took over. He brought in Noisy Nate from the cell to be a witness. Nate stood there, ratty and pale and shivering. And little by little the Sodbuster dragged the tale out of him, the ugly story of a gang who'd planned to take over the town over a year ago. How they'd bought up the town-marshal, Pell, and worked out a series of robberies and hold-ups. He accused the Marshal of encouraging Mitch Fenton to dry-gulch Appleton when he left the Bonanza. They'd not been certain that he was a detective but they figured it was safer to get him out of the way. It all came out in Nate's ugly whining voice and when he'd finished he started begging them to spare his life. I looked across at the ex-marshal but he just wasn't interested. He had already something of the dignity of a dead man.

After Noisy Nate's confession there wasn't much call for any more formalities. The jury made up its mind on the spot. They didn't even bother to listen to Morland.

'What's the verdict?' said Roper.

'Guilty as hell,' said Swede the foreman, after a rapid, whispered consultation.

'Right,' said Roper, and went on to tell Pell that the punishment was death by hanging.

'When?' Pell's voice was empty and quite calm.

'Now,' said Roper. There was something pretty tough about Roper Smith. They didn't waste any time. Someone fetched a rope and they took the former marshal of Gilburg Crossing out into the street. I went after them, something forcing me to see it through to its ugly end. I thought of Appleton and argued with myself that this was only what Pell deserved. There was a barn with a projecting beam next to the Stage office and there they took him and sat him on a horse with the noose round his neck.

Then Roper Smith, standing next to the horse, looked up and said,

'You got anything you wanta say?'

Pell shook his head. Suddenly the Sodbuster standing behind the horse lashed it with a quirt. It leapt up and forward and two seconds later Pell was hanging there, dead.

The crowd began to break up at once. Roper Smith saw me and said, 'Help me take this gold to the Stage office, Johnny. I'll feel kinda happier when it's locked up.'

When we'd stashed the gold away in Jud Larrabee's office, Roper said,

'Reckon we might go an' celebrate.'

'What?' I said. 'The coming of law and order to Gilburg Crossing?'

'That's right,' he said eagerly. It was almost as if he wanted someone to make him feel sure.

We moved across to the Bonanza where we'd first met and I had my drink, though it came nigh to choking me. Then I had to have drinks with other miners and towns-folk who all thronged into the Bonanza to drown their feeling of guilt in red-eye. There's nothing like a hanging to make folks sociable and easy to please. And then about an hour later I remembered Dan Maffrey and at once I came out in a kind of sweat of anxiety, wondering what the hell he was up to. The last picture I had of him he was walking away from the place where he'd gone down on his knees and begged Mitch

Fenton for mercy.

I said, ''Scuse me,' to Roper Smith and elbowed my way through the crowd. I got out into the street and tried to figure where he'd gone. I thought about his horse, remembering that after the posse had got back from their chase someone had offered to take the horses down to the Livery Stable. I turned down the street then, westwards. The town on that side fell away a little and before me the whole western sky was awash with crimson and gold. It was something to remember and walking down to the stable I began to feel a mite more like my ordinary self.

I reached the Livery Stable and found the liveryman lighting a lantern.

I said, 'Have you seen Dan Maffrey?'

'Who's he?' said the man.

'A big tall hombre, fair-haired, blue-eyed. Wears a blue wool shirt and a yellow bandanna round his neck. Shall I tell you about the mole on his left shoulder?'

'I seed him a half-hour back. He came in here for his hoss, bought a small sack of grain and then rode back into town. He bought a second hoss off me too.'

'I'll take my hoss,' I said. I handed him a dollar. He fetched Bessie and mounting her, we moved away up the street once more. Why had Dan Maffrey bought a second horse? It didn't make much sense. Looking at Ma Tompkins' house I thought of Jeannie and guessed she was safe and sound inside with Young Matt to watch over her. He'd do a good job of it and deep down inside me I envied him.

'She ain't for the likes of me, Bessie,' I said aloud and her ears went up as they always do when I start talking to her.

We ambled on up the street, looking for what we could find of Dan Maffrey's whereabouts. At first there was nothing to be seen. The street was empty now, shadows deepened and lights were coming on, throwing their little pools of yellow radiance out onto the dust. From the Bonanza came a steady flow of noise as miners and townsfolk celebrated the triumph of law and order. I rode past the Bonanza and came to the intersection. Lights were shining out of the Palace windows and I wondered why. Maybe Dan Maffrey had gone back there. I decided to go in and see – then I changed my mind. I rode across to the Stage office. I dismounted and slung Bessie's reins around the tie-rail. Then I saw that the door was open and tension suddenly coiled itself up in me. The miner's gold was supposed to be locked up in there.

I moved onto the boardwalk, my left hand resting on the gun in my holster. I reached the door and listened. Nothing. Not a sound. Just darkness. And then I heard something, a whisper, a faint murmur, like someone breathing with difficulty.

I spoke out into the darkness of the office, 'Who's there?' There was no reply. I decided I'd take a chance. I stepped in through the door and almost fell over something lying on the floor. I reached for my matches, struck one and held it steady. The small flame grew and looking down I saw what I'd stumbled over. It was Jud Larrabee, the stage-line agent. I looked for a lamp and found one on a desk. I lit it and had a closer look at Larrabee. Someone had put him to sleep with a pistol-barrel. He was snoring gently with a lump like an egg on his head but in no danger. I looked for the safe, half-suspecting what I'd find, and I was right. It was open and empty. The saddle-bags containing the gold were gone.

It could be Dan Maffrey, I thought. It could very well be him. He had a big grievance about all he'd lost since that day in the New Mexico desert and maybe he'd decided that this was his chance. I left Larrabee snoring on the floor and went outside. I looked across the street at the Palace, its windows all lit up but completely quiet. I went across and round the back of the saloon. Maffrey's horses were there, waiting saddled and ready. He had to be in the saloon. There wasn't anywhere else. I came back and cat-footed my way along the side of the building, past the lighted windows until I was only inches away from the batwings at the entrance. It was then that I heard a voice, the first sign of life in the big saloon. It was a voice I didn't know.

It was saying, 'That ain't the way to talk to a girl, mister.' I edged forward and had a look over the top of the nearest swing door. They were all up at the far end of the long bar – Jeannie Bain, standing there like a statue, one hand up to her throat: behind her sitting at his piano was the blind pianist, his white hair looking like the halo round the head of a saint. And standing with his back to me was Dan Maffrey, a gun in his hand. The two saddle-bags containing the gold were on the bar-top near him. He spoke while I was watching. And his voice was strange.

'You'll come with me like I said, Jeannie

Bain. I want you and I'm having you. You and the gold together. If you say no again I'll kill your young friend on the floor there.'

I knew now why he'd wanted a second horse and I knew that Matt Tompkins was in the saloon too, although what he and Jeannie were doing there I couldn't for the life of me figure out. Still, there's a time for figuring and a time for doing and this was one of the last. I'd got to do something fast.

Even as I put a hand up to the swing door to push it open, Dan Maffrey spoke again.

'Make up your mind, Miz Jeannie. Are you comin' with me?'

I pushed the door open and answered for her.

'No,' I said. 'She ain't going with you Dan.'

He whirled and stood there facing me. He was a big dangerous looking figure and in his eyes was that mad vacant look I'd seen there before.

'Keep out of this, Johnny,' he said, and his voice was not much more than a whisper. His gun still hung down from his right hand but I saw the knuckles whiten as he took a firmer grip on it and I knew the moment was not far off.

'Look, Dan,' I said, 'just hand over that

200

gold and walk out of here quiet like. Your pony's waiting. All you've got to do is ride on out of Gilburg Crossing. Head north, head south, but keep on riding.'

'Johnny,' he said, 'for a small man you're a mite too big for your boots. You're hornin' in on something you don't understand. The gold is mine and the girl is mine. They're going with me and if you don't get out of my way, I'm going to shoot you down.'

All this while Jeannie just stood there staring at us, big-eyed, and behind her the white-haired pianist sat blind-eyed at his keyboard. Matt still lay on the floor, unconscious.

I watched Dan Maffrey slowly bringing up the gun in his hand and knew it was now or never. I slapped my left hand onto the butt of my gun and drew. Dan's gun roared once, twice, and the second slug spun me round like a top. I fell, landing on my side. A bullet hit the floor not two inches from my face. I brought the gun up as I rose to a crouch and fired twice. The whole big room boomed and echoed with the explosions. I saw Dan Maffrey stagger back as my bullets hit him. For a moment he stood there swaying, a strange and terrible staring in his eyes, and then slowly he sank down to the bar-room floor. And I just stood there, knowing I had done something I would never forget.

I went over to where he had fallen and knelt down beside him. He wasn't dead, but he was dying. His eyes were no longer mad or vacant. They stared up at me almost calm and content.

'Why did you do it, Johnny?' His voice rose in a harsh whisper.

'There wasn't any other way, Dan,' I said.

'No,' he managed to whisper back. 'No other...' His voice died away, his head rolled sideways and I knew he was gone.

I went on kneeling there for a time and then I heard Jeannie speak from behind me.

'It couldn't be helped, Johnny. No one could blame you.'

I got up then and faced her. I could see Matt Tompkins sitting up on the floor touching his head with his right hand.

'No, Jeannie,' I said. 'I reckon that it had to be like that, but none the less I never wanted to be the one do it.'

'You're wounded,' she said, looking at my left shoulder, and that was the first time I remembered that Dan's second bullet had hit me. It didn't amount to much. Jeannie insisted on my taking off my shirt and there was a furrow across the top of it but nothing to make a song and dance about. However, she insisted on bandaging it, and while she did so I asked her how she and Matt had come to be in the Palace Saloon with Dan Maffrey.

It was all quite simple enough.

'Matt and I saw him riding by with a led horse when everybody was in the Bonanza. Matt couldn't figure what Dan was up to. So we decided to follow him and find out. We watched him go into the Stage office and we saw him come out with the two saddle-bags.'

She paused while tears gathered in her eyes and Matt, who'd recovered, took up the story.

'I guess I couldn't jest stand there an' let him ride off with that gold, Mr Ross. I didn't have a gun but I reckoned I could reason with him. So I slipped forward and asked him to hand over the bags an' told him he could ride on out of town if he'd do that. Howsomever that wasn't his idee at all. He pulled his gun an' herded us over to the Palace. He said we could all have a drink together before he hit the trail. Well, he got himself a drink and kept staring at Jeannie here and then he said she could go with him too. He tried to grab her an' I hit him. Then he hit me with the bar'l of his gun and I kinda lost interest.'

'Yes,' said a voice from behind us. 'That was how it was. The trouble with him was an old one. Gold. And on top of it a woman. I know all about it. I lost my eyes because of them.'

It was the blind man who spoke and he underlined what he'd said with a small tune which he picked out on the piano with one finger.

It was the tune I'd sung way back down the trail when we were riding on from Bentville, the tune about the dying cowboy and how he asked his pardners to beat the drum slowly and play the fife lowly. Well, there was no drum or fife for Dan Maffrey or for ex-marshal Pell and Fenton and Somers when we buried them next day in what was coming to be a sizeable Boot-hill just out of town. Standing there at the graveside I was just about as puzzled as ever about Dan Maffrey. He'd had his times of strength and courage, like when the Apaches came tearing down the canyon after Jeannie Bain or again in the California Hotel at Bentville. But there were others when he just didn't seem to be the same man. Times when, like at the stage coach holdup, he'd turned on me with his gun lifting and I'd figured he was mad maybe, or the time when he'd gone down on his knees to Mitch Fenton and begged for mercy, and then I'd said he was just a yellow-bellied coward.

And walking away back into town Jeannie asked the last question.

'What was wrong with Dan, Johnny?' Her voice was soft and gentle as she spoke. And there were tears in her eyes again.

I said, 'Miz Jeannie, I ain't sure at all. Maybe he was just one of those men who're neither all good or all bad, neither black nor white, just folks like you and me.'

And there we left it. An hour later I rode out of town and Jeannie and Matt waved me off. I felt kind of sad at leaving them, especially Jeannie with her light brown hair like the girl in the song. But I knew they'd be a happy married couple and there was a chance now for Gilburg Crossing with folks like them to keep it going. So I rode on north, towards Wyoming which I'd always wanted to see. I looked back once from a rise that was about half a mile out of town and saw the two small figures still standing there. Then I gave Bessie her head and rode on up the long and lonely trail. .

This Large Print Book, for people
who cannot read normal print,
is published under the auspices of

THE ULVERSCROFT FOUNDATION

... we hope you have enjoyed this book.
Please think for a moment about those
who have worse eyesight than you ...
and are unable to even read or enjoy
Large Print without great difficulty.

You can help them by sending a
donation, large or small, to:

**The Ulverscroft Foundation,
1, The Green, Bradgate Road,
Anstey, Leicestershire, LE7 7FU,
England.**
or request a copy of our brochure for
more details.

The Foundation will use all donations
to assist those people who are visually
impaired and need special attention
with medical research, diagnosis
and treatment.

Thank you very much for your help.